Abie and Arlene's Autism War

Irene Tanzman

DEDICATION

For my son, Isaac

A NOVEL INSPIRED BY MY OWN TRUE STORY

CONTENTS

ACKNOWLEDGMENTS

Many thanks to my beta readers and critiquers:
Allan Tanzman
Colleen Lutkevich
Todd Swisher

And to my inspiration
Isaac Tanzman

PART 1: BATTLE OF AUTISTIC CHILDHOOD

Chapter 1: Diagnosis and Early Intervention

Arlene's Thoughts

Abie was an infertility baby. I used thermometers, checked vaginal mucous, and did everything I could do to make my dream of a pregnancy a reality. In the end, I needed fertility drugs. Luckily, we conceived Abie the regular way. He was born healthy after an uneventful pregnancy. He weighed eight pounds and had a good strong cry. A beautiful baby boy complete with a full head of brown curly hair. He was our dream come true… a masterpiece from God in partnership with Jon and me…. and a little help from fertility pharmaceuticals. On second thought, maybe God wasn't in on it. Surely if it were God's will, I would have gotten pregnant without pills.

As a newborn, Abie had a very strange stare. He gazed blankly and straight on with wide eyes. From the beginning, he nursed funny. Sometimes he seemed to know just what to do… just like other babies. Other times he seemed to be drifting off in space. This pattern followed him as he grew older. Sometimes he seemed to

1

know exactly what was going on. He even seemed insightful at times. At other times, he totally tuned out the world, and it was impossible to break through. As he grew, all his motor skills were on time, but I knew there was something off about his development.

"Abie doesn't talk," I told the pediatrician.

"He's too young to talk," he replied.

It wasn't just that he didn't talk. He wasn't developing the prerequisites for talking. He didn't have a social smile or the social back and forth like other babies. He didn't raise his arms to be picked up out of his crib, or cry when I wasn't in his view.

I knew I should be talking to him in order to facilitate his development. I talked plenty, but he didn't receive my words. When the dentist performed surgery on my gums, I was secretly relieved to have a convenient excuse not to talk to him. He was non-responsive. He didn't play with rattles or toys. He was only interested in a plant I had in the living room. He shook the plant for hours on end. When he began to walk, he went from walking to running in a matter of days. He ran back and forth as if in an unbreakable trance. He was in his own world in his endless quest to pace at lightning speed. Still he was my baby, and I loved him. Sometimes I think I didn't love him enough or give him the right attention. Maybe if I had, he would have been a miracle autistic genius, the kind they write about in books and articles.

He acquired some words, and then I reassured myself. Then he lost those words as fast as he acquired them. I expressed my concerns to the pediatrician dozens of times.

The pediatrician recommended preschool. "Sometimes when parents anticipate their child's wants and needs, this can affect speech development." According to him, Abie was perfectly normal. My mothering was causing his problems. All he needed was some time away from me. Once in preschool, he would be speaking in no time.

In preschool, it became painstakingly obvious there was something wrong with him. All I needed to do was compare him to the other children. "Give him some time in the preschool, and it will all work out. He doesn't need testing. He's perfectly normal," said the pediatrician.

Against his orders, I went to the local children's hospital to have him tested at age two and a half. Just to make sure, I brought him to two different neurologists to confirm the diagnosis. At first, the diagnosis was something called "PDD." Diagnosticians sometimes prefer to give PDD as a diagnosis instead of autism. "PDD not otherwise specified" is supposed to be milder than autism, but Abie had the symptoms of severe classic autism. They just didn't want to say it. Some parents have no clue as to what PDD actually is. It stands for "pervasive developmental disorder." Doesn't sound too good, but if you just use the PDD alphabet soup, it sounds like a variation of ADHD or something less than what it is. One neurologist actually did give him the autism diagnosis. My husband, Jon, knew that PDD meant autism for Abie, and cried like a baby when we received the diagnosis.

The reaction of friends and family was unhelpful for the most part.

"You let him get attached to his blankie. That's why he has problems."

"I have a doctor you can take him to. This doctor is a miracle worker. He'll cure Abie."

"Everybody has problems. God only gives you problems that you can handle. When He closes the door, He opens a window."

"Sorry about that. Did I tell you how my little Josh is so smart and advanced for his age?"

"You took fertility drugs. When you try to go against God's wishes, things like this happen."

"You're being punished for sins you committed in a previous life."

"Bad parenting causes autism. I don't think that you gave him enough attention."

There was the one statement I kept on hearing over and over again. "If you work intensively with a kid with autism for thirty or forty hours a week, you can cure him. But the intervention must be before the age of five." This almost sounded like an antidote to a witch's spell in a fairy tale. And yes, I believed it. It's hard to say if I continued to believe it as our journey went on. I did know some children who had a marked increase in functioning level in the preschool years. However, it was impossible to obtain the intensive thirty hour a week teaching back then. You could try to do it yourself or if you were very wealthy, you could finance it.

I knew I needed to get busy even though I could only obtain less than the ideal intervention. I had no time to feel sorry for my family and myself. There was too much to do.

I made a call to early intervention. They assigned a service coordinator to us. Her name was Terri Clearway. "At last I'll be getting some help. Maybe she'll give me just the direction I need," I thought. I prayed Terri would be our angel.

She called me the next day. I can still hear her enthusiastic voice. "Hi, I'm Terri Clearway from the Newtucktin Guidance Center. I'm returning your call from yesterday. I want to set up a time to meet Abie and discuss an individual family service plan. How about next week?"

We made the appointment. Terri showed up dressed in a beautiful coordinated designer business suit complete with pinstripes and a white silk blouse. She was a slender businesslike woman in her mid-forties with neatly coiffed brown hair and a strong confident stride. I was in black sweat pants and a dirty pink sweatshirt. My hair was unkempt, and my fingernails were dirty from trying to clean some mud off the floor. I was only thirty years old, but I looked at least fortyish, maybe even fiftyish. I was often mistaken for Abie's grandmother. I had at least fifty extra pounds from a combination of stress and baby weight. My house was a mess with items strewn around. Abie had a tendency to take things out of draws and cabinets. Crumbs decorated the floor. Terri looked at Abie for roughly fifteen minutes while keeping at least ten feet away from him. "I agree with the diagnosis of PDD…actually it's more like a full blown case of classic autism. We'll see what we can do for you. I'll call you next week." Terri didn't try to interact with Abie during the entire time she was there.

I waited with anticipation for Terri's call. Finally, the phone rang. It was Terri.

"I'm going to match you up with a wonderful therapist for Abie. Her name is Marilyn, and she's an expert in Down's syndrome."

"Abie doesn't have Down's syndrome. He has autism. You said so yourself."

"Oh, there isn't all that much difference between all of these disabilities. I wouldn't worry too much about that. An expert is an expert, and Marilyn has many skills. Also, since Abie is so close to age three, you might want to call up your school district and see about a school placement for him."

At that time, I knew nothing about what early intervention or the school district was obligated to provide. In the early 1990s most people didn't have access to much information. This was before the age of the internet.

According to federal law, when a child transitions out of early intervention, the early intervention team must prepare the child for transition into school services. The transition to a school program isn't something parents must arrange without assistance. According to our state regulations, early intervention must take the lead to make this happen smoothly by holding a transition-planning meeting. I was ignorant of early intervention's responsibilities. Terri Clearway knew this and took full advantage.

I also asked Terri, "Is there a way to access trained caregivers to watch Abie while I look at possible school programming for him?"

"As far as I know, nothing like that exists. Sorry." Respite services were available through the state. Terri Clearway was either ignorant of that fact, or wasn't interested in providing information on how to access this.

With a confirmed diagnosis in hand, I read everything I could about autism and PDD. I read *Son Rise,* a book about a boy who fully recovered from his autistic condition. I learned about the Lovaas experiments using operant conditioning, the precursor to ABA or applied behavior analysis. Supposedly Lovaas was able to return 47 percent of children he treated into mainstream classrooms. I read repeatedly…..the earlier and more intense the intervention, the better chance Abie would have. Therefore, it was a race against the clock. Early intervention was my hope. I couldn't wait for Marilyn to arrive at my door.

Marilyn showed up in casual clothing, and no jewelry. Freedom of movement was just what she needed to chase around toddlers in motion. Jewelry would have easily distracted her toddler learners. No sense in wearing earrings anyway. Someone might try to rip those off her ear. She wasn't old. Maybe she was about age 30, young enough to have the flexibility to get up and down from a chair made for little kids. She carried a black bag with a variety of toys in it. One toy was a basket with blocks. Another was rings of different sizes on a stick. When she arrived at my house, Abie, as usual, was running back and forth. He paid no attention to her.

"I have a child size table with little chairs in Abie's room where you can work. Would you like to sit there or is it better to sit at the kitchen table?"

"The little table would be better for the intervention. You'll have to bring Abie there."

I picked him up and broke his running ritual. He screamed as if his life depended on it. The cries got louder and louder as I sat him on the little chair. He did everything to try to get away and get back to what he was doing, but I held him in his chair. Marilyn sat down in a child-sized chair, and pulled out the basket and blocks.

"Mrs. Dancer, fill and pour is an important skill for toddlers to learn. This is a prerequisite for toilet training among other things. They normally learn on their own, but sometimes they don't. That's where early intervention comes in. We can teach this."

Marilyn put her hands over Abie's hands and made him grasp the blocks one by one to fill the basket. As she forced him to place each block into the basket, his cries got louder and louder. He flailed and tried to break free from her grasp. He tried to get out of the chair, but I held him back. "There were twenty blocks in all. Each one was more tortuous than the previous. After they placed all the blocks in the basket, Marilyn put her hands over Abie's hands and dumped the blocks back on the table. Then she shouted, "Yay. Good job, Abie." He let out a loud wail as she did this. I had a terrible feeling in the pit of my stomach while I thought, "So this is the intervention. Something doesn't seem right."

"Mrs. Dancer, Abie needs a break. I'm going to let him go." He ran off and continued his endless running back and forth for several paces. Then he ran over to the plant and shook it incessantly. The clock was ticking away. Soon it would be time for Marilyn to leave, so I grabbed Abie out of his trance. As I took him away from the plant, he tried to bite my wrist, but I was able to avoid it. I told Marilyn she needed to be careful to avoid a possible bite to her wrist as she worked with him with the rings on the stick.

Marilyn positioned her hands over his hands to force him to complete the rings on a stick. He screamed as she forced him to place the rings on the stick starting with the largest ring. When that task was over, I asked Marilyn if she ever used food rewards to get the children to comply.

"I don't believe in that. That's how we train dogs and cats. It's not for people."

"That's what they did in *Son Rise*. Lovaas did that too. I'd like to have the same kind of results they talk about."

"There are all sorts of claims out there. You have to be careful about what you believe in."

At that point, I didn't know what to think. Our session was

over, so I led her to the door. "Thank you. See you at the service plan meeting on Monday. Marilyn, how often are you going to be visiting us?"

"I'll be coming once a week for an hour. We'll explain all of that at our meeting for the Individual Family Service Plan meeting. We call it the IFSP."

"Once a week! But I read that a kid like Abie needs about forty hours of intense intervention."

"We can only provide once a week treatment for Abie. That is what they recommended back at the Newtucktin Guidance Center. Our intervention is top quality. You won't find any better than us."

I was shocked they thought once a week intervention would help Abie catch up. I thought, "Maybe he's less impaired than I think…they're the professionals. They know more than I do, and more than what I read. After all, this is their field, what they studied in college. I should trust in them, but then again, maybe I shouldn't." I guess I was confused. The following week I had the individual family service plan meeting with Terri and Marilyn. I signed the plan without protest even though I had a funny feeling about what they were giving us. Jon had to take care of Abie, so he didn't come to the meeting.

When Marilyn came the following Thursday, it was a repeat of the previous week. There was no progress.

As my frustration set in, I asked Marilyn, "How much experience do you have with working with children diagnosed with PDD or autism?"

"I've done a lot of work with Down's syndrome children. Not too much work with PDD or autism. The office refers most of them to autism specialty services. "

The remark hit me like a knife in my stomach. "SPECIALTY SERVICES! That's probably what we need. How do we get that?"

"I don't think you can get that now. You already signed the service plan, and you only have a few months left of early intervention anyway. You're probably better off trying to figure out how to get him into a good school placement."

I felt cheated. They had an autism specialty service available, but they didn't tell us about it or offer it to us.

I thought it would be better to switch to the topic of a school placement. I was on the verge of exploding over the fact that nobody offered Abie access to specialty services.

"What do you know about school placements? The hospital said I should be fighting for a private placement. What do you think?"

"If the public school can't handle Abie, they have to pay for a private school that can. The schools hesitate to send students to these private placements because they aren't cheap. If you want a private placement, you might need a lawyer. Whether or not Abie needs a private placement depends on what the school offers you. Look at what they propose, and then you can make a decision. I can tell you what I know about the private placements around here. I've seen the two main private specialty school programs for young children with PDD or autism."

"The two programs I heard about were the Behavioral School and Cognitive Kids," I said.

"Yup. Those are the two. I was very uncomfortable with what I saw at the Behavioral School. They use seclusion and restraint, and a disconcerting heads down procedure. The other one, Cognitive Kids, is run by a guy who's very anti-behavior modification. They use a lot of signing, but they don't use official ASL, so I'm not sure how practical that is. Also, it's in an iffy neighborhood, and it's a bitch to find parking around there. You could try calling them. They might be your best bet."

Neither option seemed too appealing to me, but I called Cognitive Kids. They gave Abie and me an appointment in three weeks with a woman named Elsa. She would give Abie a trial therapy session and introduce me to their method.

In the meantime, I tried to engage Abie in ANYTHING. I couldn't get his attention or eye contact. I couldn't break through. It seemed hopeless. Jon thought I should place my trust in Marilyn, and not use food rewards. After three consecutive sessions with Marilyn and no progress, I decided to go against Marilyn's wishes and Jon's wishes. I used pieces of Abie's favorite crackers to get him to place the blocks in the basket. We did the task over and over again. First with crying. Then with no crying. First with hand over hand. Then he did it himself in order to get the pieces of crackers. Little by little, I gave him fewer and fewer crackers until he could do the task without getting the crackers. The whole process took hundreds of hours, but I felt I was on my way with Abie. I finally felt some hope, but the hope was about to multiply when I met Elsa at Cognitive Kids.

Elsa was a middle-aged woman. She had back-to-back appointments with toddlers diagnosed with PDD. For the life of me, I don't know how she found the energy. In later times, her clientele would have looked similar but probably would have carried the diagnosis of autism spectrum disorder or ASD. In the back room, she had piles of clothing she used when toddlers peed on her, pooped on her, tore her clothing, or for other mishaps. Cognitive Kids was in the poorest section of town. Bringing Abie to Cognitive Kids made me an expert on parallel parking in very tight spaces.

Inside the broken down building was a group of rooms on the first floor for the toddler program. The softly painted rooms had a calming effect. There were various therapy sessions going on. You could hear some laughter and happy sounds coming out of the rooms. I also heard a few odd sounds called self-stimulatory noises. Individuals diagnosed with autism tend to make these noises. The happy sounds were louder, and I heard no screaming or crying. I thought to myself, "This is more like it."

Elsa smiled wide, stooped down to Abie's height, and spoke in a strong Swedish accent. "Well, hello, little Abie. They told me you were coming, but they didn't tell me you would be this cute." Then she looked up at me. "Mrs. Dancer, Abie is a doll!"

She made her voice go louder and softer as she watched how Abie would respond. She moved close to his face as she made noises and then pulled back. She did this several times. Not only did she get Abie to produce eye contact, but he also laughed as if he was enjoying what she was doing with him. She brought out a bucket of rice for him to pour. He stared at the rice as if pouring rice was the most interesting thing in the world. Then she swung Abie in her arms, and sang playfully "Here you go! Swinging! Swinging! Up and down Abie!"

Then she stopped swinging and started kissing and hugging Abie. "Did you have fun? Like the swinging?" He laughed and smiled with joy when she did this. I was surprised because he usually didn't like strangers to touch him. It was astounding to see him so engaged. By the end of the session, I knew this was what I wanted for him. I could feel this working. I asked about having regular sessions with Elsa.

Abie met with Elsa three times a week for an hour and with Marilyn once a week until he turned 3 years old. I also made an appointment with Dr. Smith, the founder of Cognitive Kids and the Cognitive Kids method. The purpose of this appointment was to evaluate Abie and discuss a possible school placement at Cognitive Kids for him when he turned age three.

Dr. Smith emphasized the relationship between the child and the parent. It was important for Abie to notice me, to have eye contact with me, to attach to me, and to have the back and forth a baby might have with a parent. In years past, Bruno Bettelheim's poor parenting theories accused mothers of autistic children of sabotaging the parent-child attachment. I didn't agree with Bettelheim's theories, but I thought the attachment between primary caretaker and child was very important. These were the beginning skills and the groundwork for language… but how do you do this with a toddler who won't even look at you?

"Tickle him. Kiss him. Hug him. Roughhouse him. He enjoys

a swinging motion… so swing him. Maybe swing him in a blanket. Enjoy him. Just do whatever you can do to get him to look at you naturally. Get him to want to look at you," said Elsa.

The four hours of intervention Abie received per week was very different from the thirty or forty hours he needed according to what I read. I was supplementing his days with many hours of my intervention. I did whatever I could to try to intervene. I did as Elsa recommended. I used my intuition and the information I gleaned from reading books. I cheated. I used food rewards. I did what they told me, and what I thought they would tell me if they knew more. I couldn't get my hands on enough reading material on PDD or on autism. I read whatever I could. I had hope. Abie would beat the odds. He would be normal. We would make him normal. We would cure him. He would lead a normal life. A job. Marriage. Kids.

Abie's Thoughts

If you want to know what I was like as a little kid, I was a retard. That says it all. Many people called me a retard… so that's what I was. Do you hate me yet?

I was… something bad, something less than what normal people are. I was a special kind of retard called an autistic. Back then, they also called me a PDD uneducable low functioning autistic retard.

Sometimes words are so bad that people can't say them. You're not supposed to say the word, "fuck," so you say "F-ing" instead. PDD is just like a fuck word. You're not allowed to say those words. You're not allowed to say the word the P stands for, and the word the D stands for, and the word the other D stands for. So instead, you just say the bunch of letters. Maybe those letters stand for Pest who is Dumber than Dirt. Whatever it is, it's so bad that you just can't say it, just like you can't say "fuck"

Some autistics do funny things like flap their hands in front of their faces; make loud noises or lineup, flip, or spin things. Real people call this "stimming." I love stimming. That makes me bad, and it makes me a retard. Real people will do anything to try to stop a retard from stimming.

Many real people say I'm a drain on society. I don't know why they think that. I look nothing like a drain. A drain has many holes so water can go down and disappear. Some real people wish I would disappear. Maybe that's why.

I do know I caused a lot of trouble....and I mean a LOT OF TROUBLE. And speaking of drains... once I took Mommy's money and threw it all down the drain. I loved the way I'd see the money, and then the money would disappear down the drain. She had to call the plumber because of that. I caused a lot of trouble around drains. Maybe they called me "drain" because I did that.

Mommy wasn't happy when I threw her money down the drain, but she didn't cry. I can tell you about a time she did cry. Once I found twenty pieces of paper in her bedroom. I ripped up those papers into tiny little pieces. Then I threw them into the air and watched them fly around the room. Mommy was in the bathroom so she couldn't stop me. When she came out, she found me having a wonderful time in her room. She cried and screamed. "Our taxes, our taxes! I've been working on them for days!" When I got older, I still liked to rip up pieces of paper, throw them in the air, and say, "a taxi, a taxi, four yays!" When I said that, I thought about the good time I had when I found all those papers.

Do you know who real people are? They're all the people who aren't retards. Those people are real and normal. Retards aren't really people, nor are they animals. They're something a little worse than an animal. Real people are worried about other real people hurting animals, but they aren't worried about real people hurting retards. Retards get hurt all the time in schools and in programs for grown up retards, but nobody does anything about it. It's okay to hurt a retard, but it's not okay to hurt a dog or a cat. Also, it's okay for a dog to bark loudly and disturb the neighbors, but it isn't okay for a retard to have loud stim noises. It just isn't.

Some people think a retard like me can't remember anything. But the truth is …I remember everything. I remember too much. I remember way back when. I remember what real people forgot. But… I remember only important things.

For instance, when Mommy makes chicken… I see her putting away leftovers. I want to get those leftovers. I never forget they're there in the refrigerator. I want someone to give them to me. I'll kick the refrigerator if I have to. That's why there are so many dents in the refrigerator and the walls. I'm very annoying. Most retards are either annoying or a drain on society. I'm both those things. Anyway, if Mommy doesn't give me leftovers, I steal them when she unlocks the refrigerator. I'm very fast and clever. I had a lot of practice stealing. I know how to steal quickly. Nobody notices until it's too late, and I already have what I want. Isn't that funny…. a clever retard? Everyone knows a retard is supposed to be stupid!

Mommy once took me to a house. They gave me chocolate cake with chocolate frosting. Five years later, when she took me to that same house, I wanted chocolate cake again. After all, that was the chocolate cake house. They had some delicious cookies they offered me, but I was angry, raving mad, pissed off, and righteous indignation. In the chocolate cake house, they should have chocolate cake…not cookies. They said I melted down. I saw the green wicked witch melting down on TV, and it was awful. I definitely didn't want that happening to me. I guess Mommy got me out of there just in time. So that's why we can never go back to the chocolate cake house again. Such a shame! Those people were nice, and their cookies were delicious.

Real people want to know why I forgot words when I was young. First, I had words, and then those words disappeared. Did I forget the words? No, I never forgot any words. The words I had then weren't words at all. They weren't words because I didn't know what words were. I didn't know everything had a name. I didn't know the sounds people made when talking to each other were people talking to each other. I thought people were just making sounds…..just like when the refrigerator or the air conditioner makes sounds. The words I had were just random sounds I heard and felt like repeating. They had no meaning. They weren't important to remember. So I said them, and then I didn't say them.

I remember what happened to me when I was young….. very young. I remember colors, sounds, shapes, smells, and the feelings I had when I touched something or when someone or something touched me. Everything was loud, overly bright, confusing, overwhelming, hurtful, and scary. I couldn't make sense of it all, so I did whatever I could do to blank out everything. I just wanted to be alone. Whenever I had trouble blocking out the world, I cried.

I loved shaking Mommy's big plant. I could see the green leaves sway back and forth. It made me feel good. I also loved to run back and forth over and over again. As I ran, I saw colors and shapes and I felt air against my face even in the inside of the house. There was no reason to figure out what the colors and shapes meant. But real people like Mommy wanted me to know what they meant.

I remember Marilyn, the woman from early intervention. Marilyn and Mommy wanted me to stop stimming and do other things. But those things were confusing and scary, and stimming was fun. I cried, and tried to get away from them and the evil thing that they were trying to do. I was happy to get back to my running and my plant when it was over.

Around that time, Mommy kept a stash of the white crackers with salt on them. She gave me little pieces of these crackers. I liked crackers, and I liked eating. She gave me crackers for placing the blocks in the basket. I knew eventually I would get crackers for figuring out the blocks in a basket.

After much practice, I knew when I saw a basket; I was supposed to put blocks in it. After a while, Mommy stopped giving me crackers to put the blocks into the basket. I just put the blocks into the basket because it felt like the right thing to do.

I remember Mommy taking me to Elsa. I remember Elsa moving really close to me, then moving far from me over and over again. When she was in the best spot, she stopped. She talked loud. She talked soft. She talked in-between. She figured out what type of sounds I liked. Elsa was able to figure out what I liked to do, what I liked to smell, what I liked to hear, what I wanted to feel through my fingertips, what I wanted to see, and where I wanted to move about. But she wasn't able to get me to understand everything that was so loud, so confusing, and so scary.

Dr. Smith tried to test me, but I wasn't going to do the scary things he wanted me to do. I wasn't even going to try. After all, he wasn't giving me crackers or anything. Why should I? Because I didn't do what Dr Smith told me, he said I was very impaired and low functioning. That meant I was a retard who was one of the worst retards you can think of, and it probably wasn't worthwhile to try to teach me much of anything because I wouldn't understand it.

Dr. Smith asked Mommy to walk out of the room to see if I'd follow her. Many other times I wouldn't run after Mommy, but this time I ran right after her. I thought she'd protect me from this Smith man who was trying to force me to do so many things I didn't want to do. Dr. Smith, Elsa, and Mommy were very happy when I did that. They all said I had an attachment to Mommy. This showed "promise." I swear... Mommy and I didn't have a rope or a string or scotch tape or anything else that attached us to each other. Also, I made no promises.

Chapter 2: The School Placement

B y the time we came close to Abie's third birthday, my enthusiasm for teaching Abie many hours a day was waning. I was tired and worn out. I needed a break so badly I could scream. At age three, he would become eligible for a therapeutic school placement in accordance with the Individuals with Disabilities Education Act, better known by the initials, IDEA. I couldn't wait for that to happen. I'd get a break, and Abie could finally get the help he desperately needed. The thought of a school placement filled me with optimism and hope.

The liaison from the Newtucktin school district, Mary Carpenter, asked me to bring Abie in for evaluation at a nearby public school program. She thought this program might possibly be an appropriate placement for him. It sounded good. It was only five minutes from my house. The program had six preschoolers in it with developmental disabilities, and six preschoolers who had no disabilities. They called this kind of program "an integrated classroom" because it contained both disabled and nondisabled students. Mary Carpenter described the classroom in detail, but she couldn't get me an opportunity for an observation just yet. At this point, I was more interested in having Abie at Cognitive Kids when

17

he turned age three, but I thought I should be open to the possibility of having him in his home district. After all, it would be better for him to be in his own neighborhood, his own community. I was excited and hopeful this program might be a good fit for Abie.

Jean Tremblay came booming into the room after the receptionist announced our arrival. She looked like a fancy lady who was just about to embark on a shopping spree at Lord and Taylor's. She was wearing a blue linen pantsuit and myriads of jewelry. She smelled like she had bathed in perfume. With her nose in the air and a sour look on her face, she acted as if Abie and I were lower than chewed up gum she might have erroneously stepped on. "I'm the special education expert working for the Newtucktin school district. I'm also the overseer of the integrated program for preschoolers at this location. I'm going to test Abie."

She didn't greet Abie or talk to him directly. I didn't think she could handle him alone in a room for ten minutes, much less get him to do anything for her. After about five minutes, she came out of the room dragging him by the hand as if he were a heavy piece of trash. She had a mean and nasty look on her face. She pulled Purell out of a drawer and rubbed it into her hands all the way up to the elbow. Abie looked angry and unhappy.

"This child is very impaired. He has no skills and is so low functioning that I can't even test him." She was clearly annoyed that Mary Carpenter had referred us to her. Our existence also seemed to annoy her.

"Abie's working with Elsa Dubion over at Cognitive Kids. He also works with Marilyn Taylor from the Newtucktin Guidance Center. Perhaps you could call them to get a better idea of his skill level," I said.

She looked at me with a disgusted face. "Calling those people won't be necessary. I'm an expert, and I have a very good idea of what we're dealing with. There are a few more professionals who need to see your child, but right now, I have to get back to work." Then she raised her nose and walked off without saying goodbye.

A week later, Mary Carpenter called. "Jean Tremblay's classroom isn't appropriate for Abie, but I have a perfect placement for him in a multi-handicapped classroom."

I didn't know what to think. But there was one thing I knew for sure. I needed help and advice from people who had more experience than I did. I called every organization in the telephone book and searched for a support group for parents of children with disabilities. I hoped to find peers who might be able to advise me on some of these decisions. One support group met weekly during the day, but I couldn't attend. Who would take care of Abie? Finally, I found a support group that held meetings in the evening. Jon watched Abie while I attended. Although I was concerned as to how Jon would survive taking care of Abie, I needed to learn and network with other parents. I prayed Abie would sleep while I attended the group.

I met Jayne Johnson at this Tuesday night support group. The Newtucktin school district had placed her son, Ethan, at the Butcher Street multi-handicapped classroom. This was the placement the district was considering for Abie. When I told her about the district's proposal, she opened her mouth wide into an O. "Wow. I have …A LOT TO TELL YOU." I was at the edge of my seat wanting to hear what Jayne Johnson had to say.

The social worker, Claire Aber, who was leading the meeting said, "I have several items on the agenda to discuss. We need to bring this meeting to order." She made a speech about the benefits of networking among parents. Her speech lasted fifty minutes. Finally, we had the last ten minutes to talk to each other.

"The Butcher Street multi-handicapped program is totally inappropriate for our children. The peer group is children with profound disabilities. They can't walk or move around. Our kids need physical exercise. Those kids have other needs. Most of them are medically fragile. It's dangerous to have those children together with our autistic kids who might do something like rip out a feeding tube. They want to place our kids there because they have an opening to fill. Open slots cost money," said Jayne.

"Don't they have a program for kids like ours?"

"No, they don't. The Newtucktin School district is moving towards "full inclusion," but in truth, it's anything but "full inclusion." They're concentrating on serving students who can be mainstreamed within the district. But they'd never consider mainstreaming kids as impaired as ours. They're disbanding their substantially separate classrooms. There's only a few left. They're trying to dump everyone in what's left whether or not the placement is appropriate. I'm getting Ethan out. He's going to Cognitive Kids. I have a name of a lawyer who can help you."

"I'll take that name. I think you told me what I wanted to know. Thank you so much." Jayne also told me about obtaining respite services for Abie. She said I might get funding for respite, but I'd have to find and train my own respite person. I wondered how the respite agencies got away with just cutting checks, and not doing any hiring or training. I made a mental note to ask Elsa if she knew anyone who could do respite for me. Later Elsa gave me the name of a young woman, Maureen Pauley, who worked at Cognitive Kids, but was in the process of taking another job at the Behavioral School.

The next day I called Mary Carpenter. I told her I wanted Abie placed at Cognitive Kids. Mary replied, "I'm not sure Cognitive Kids is an appropriate placement for Abie. We want to have the best fit possible. We're the professionals, and we know precisely how to match a student up with the best intervention and the most optimal peer group. We have your son's best interests in mind."

After my discussion with Jayne Johnson, I didn't believe a word Mary Carpenter said. I called the lawyer whom Jayne recommended. Her name was Leila Fine. She wanted to know what the recommendations were from the evaluation from Children's Hospital. She stopped me when I read, "We recommend that Abraham Dancer be placed in a year-round thirty hour a week therapeutic program that specializes in autism." She cried, "STOP THERE." Then she shouted, "THAT'S JUST WHAT WE NEED. The multi-handicapped school program is probably not year round. It's also not a specialty program for autism. This report will help us a great deal."

A week later, I received a telephone call from a very excited and out of breath Jayne Johnson. "Arlene, I'm so happy for you and Abie! I think you're going to get that placement at Cognitive Kids! I kept in touch with the teacher from the multi-handicapped classroom. The higher ups wanted to place another autistic kid in her classroom and she told them, "NO. If you do that, I'm walking." She must have been talking about Abie. This means YOU PROBABLY GOT THE PLACEMENT WITHOUT A DUE PROCESS HEARING! Maybe Mary Carpenter will call you soon to tell you. Congratulations! I am so happy for you."

It was funny to hear "congratulations" in connection with Abie getting a placement in a school for children with disabilities. In another context someone might have said, "So sorry that your kid has to go to that school instead of a normal school." I thought, "is this something to celebrate... having your son go to a school in a neighborhood far away instead of having the chance to be in his own school in his own neighborhood?"

By then, I had been educated somewhat. I knew many families had to pay thousands of dollars to lawyers and advocates to get an appropriate school placement...so maybe it was something to celebrate. I thanked Jayne. I was fortunate she had the inside scoop and was willing to share this information. Soon Abie would have a thirty hour a week placement at Cognitive Kids. It was a relief to know.

That very day Mary Carpenter called. "Mrs. Dancer, I had a meeting with my superiors. I told them of your desire to have Abie attend Cognitive Kids. We want to respect your wishes, so we've decided to fund your son's placement there instead of placing him at the Butcher Street School. As you know, the team meeting is in a few weeks. You don't plan to have anyone at the meeting besides yourself and your husband. Is that correct?"

Mary didn't know I had the inside scoop about the real reason we were getting this placement. It made me shudder to realize how easily Mary Carpenter lied.

"As a matter of fact, I do plan to bring my attorney," I said.

"An attorney is not necessary. The Newtucktin School Department is going to honor your request to have Abie placed at Cognitive Kids."

"Thank you very much, but I need representation for the first team meeting. I'm sure you understand."

"Actually, I don't understand. Having a lawyer at a team meeting such as this pits you against the school district. I was hoping we could act as a team. A lawyer is adversarial. This will interfere with your relationship with the school. Remember your relationship with the district is going to be long term. You want it to be a good one. It's also unnecessary to bring a lawyer because we've agreed to your demands. These demands, mind you, are going to be very expensive for the district, but we're agreeing to them anyway. We're acting in good faith, and we hope you'll reciprocate by doing the same. We're doing everything possible to facilitate the relationship between you and the district."

I thought about what Mary said for a moment. Then I thought about the one hour a week early intervention was providing us. Jon and I were paying for the intervention at Cognitive Kids. I was working very hard putting in numerous hours teaching Abie. Others had several hours of service at Cognitive Kids or at the Behavioral School Home Program paid by early intervention specialty services. Early Intervention was not providing the services to Abie that others were getting. I never knew why. This time I wanted him to receive the best I could get. But then again, the district had already agreed to the placement at Cognitive Kids. What could possibly go wrong?

"Please think about whether or not you want to bring a lawyer. I strongly advise against it. It's not a good idea. It's a needless expense for you. You have a few weeks to think about it. You can always cancel the lawyer at the last minute if you don't need representation," said Mary.

"Okay. I'll think about it, but I might still be bringing the lawyer. Her name is Leila Fine."

The team meeting occurred two weeks before Abie's third birthday in April. I didn't know what to expect. I was happy Jon and I decided to include Leila Fine at the meeting. I saw no reason to inform the district about our plans to bring Leila. They assumed we wouldn't bring her.

I counted the days until the meeting. My house was a mess while I spent hours on end working with Abie. He was often up much of the night, so I had little sleep. I was mentally and physically exhausted. It was like running a marathon that went on for months at a time and never stopped. What kept me going was soon, Abie would be in school thirty hours per week. I'd still work with him after school and on weekends, but I'd have some time to clean up the house, do laundry, do shopping, and take a much needed break. I felt like I was drowning.

When the educational team has a meeting to write an individual educational plan, parents and professionals refer to the meeting as an "IEP team meeting." Under IDEA, those who are eligible for special education services are entitled to a free and appropriate education tailored to the individual's unique needs.

Jon, Leila, and I walked into the team meeting that day. We were surprised to see ten women sitting at the long rectangular table. Each woman had a huge stack of papers in front of her. I wondered how those stacks of papers got so large. Each person who tested Abie said he had no skills. So how much can you write about nothing?

This was the first time I met Mary Carpenter in person although I spoke to her many times on the phone. Mary Carpenter was a woman in her mid-thirties, well-dressed in an expensive looking gray suit.

She began the meeting with introductions, and a sign in sheet. The nine other people representing the school district were a speech therapist, an occupational therapist, a school psychologist, a physical therapist, a social worker, a behavior consultant, an early childhood education specialist, a curriculum specialist and a special education teacher. A few people at the table had tried to test Abie. Others read the reports and were there to lend their "expert opinions."

When Leila Fine introduced herself as the attorney representing Abraham Dancer and his family, Mary Carpenter shot us a nasty look. There were only twelve chairs around the table. We had to scrounge around to borrow a chair from another room.

Mary began the meeting. "We've received detailed reports from early intervention. I'm pleased to say Abraham Dancer has met several of his early intervention goals. He can now do a fill and pour task. When he first started early intervention services with Marilyn Taylor, he was resistant. At that time, he cried and resisted sitting at the table. He started with full hand-over-hand prompts. Now he sits nicely at the table for the duration of the task, and places the blocks into the basket independently. At the start of early intervention, he had no eye contact whatsoever. Now he has some occasional eye contact."

She went on. "Since Abraham has done so well with early intervention, we propose that he stays in early intervention until the beginning of the school year. In September, the Newtucktin School District will place Abraham at Cognitive Kids as the parents have requested. All ten of us here representing the school district have agreed this is the best course of action. Therefore, there is a consensus of the entire IEP team. We'll continue to pay for the individual service plan of one hour of service per week, and use the plan early intervention created until September. At that time, we'll have Cognitive Kids draw up a new IEP for Abraham. So now, if I can have the family sign right here, we can adjourn this meeting and the Dancers can go out and enjoy this wonderful day we're having." Then she shuffled some papers and placed a sheet in front of me to sign.

I sat upright in my chair as my pulse beat faster. I wasn't expecting this.

Jon stared at her. "Cognitive Kids has an opening for Abie now. We don't know that they'll have an opening in September."

"The Newtucktin School District is responsible for placing Abie. If there's no spot at Cognitive Kids, it'll be incumbent on us to find him another placement. We're prepared to take that risk. You don't have to worry. He can't go unserved according to the law," said Mary.

I tried to compose myself. "From everything that I've read, it's imperative that a young child diagnosed with autism receive intense early intervention before the age of five....about thirty hours a week."

"Mrs. Dancer, it's unrealistic to think someone would be able to engage Abie thirty hours a week. You need to accept the extent of your child's impairment. Your child is in good hands, and we want to continue that. We're the professionals, and we all agree." I looked around at everyone representing the school district. They were all nodding in a reticent way.

Then Leila finally rescued us. "Abie Dancer has global delays. He's about to turn three years old. He has no language or play behavior. The Children's Hospital recommended that Abie receive thirty hours of intense intervention per week year round. Cognitive Kids can provide these hours of intervention. I don't see anything in your reports that indicates one hour a week is sufficient. I also don't believe your recommendations will hold up at a due process hearing. We'll initiate a hearing if we don't get the placement with Cognitive Kids starting April 25th when Abie turns three."

"Abraham is making effective progress. Our school year starts in September, not April. What you propose is not the way that we normally do things," replied Mary.

"Well, maybe it is about time that you did things according to the law," Leila said flatly.

Mary's demeanor changed to anger for a second, but she composed herself and smiled a phony looking smile. "It'll be a hassle for Mrs. Dancer to drive Abie back and forth every day to Cognitive Kids. There's no rush here. Is there?" Then she turned to me. "Wouldn't you rather have him at home for a little longer, or would you rather hand him over to strangers as soon as you can? After all, he's just a toddler."

I was about to reply when Leila spoke. "According to the law, the district is responsible for Abie's transportation. This should be included in the service grid. In addition, sending him to a therapeutic preschool is hardly giving up parenting responsibilities. I would venture to say that some of you at this very meeting might have your children in daycare forty hours a week or more. Are you handing over your children to strangers as soon as you can?" Leila looked around at the professionals around the room. Nobody spoke.

Mary began to look defeated. "I don't have the authority to make financial decisions for the district. This will cost more money than we planned. I need to have approval from my superiors to make such decisions."

"Then what are you doing leading a team meeting in the first place? We're entitled to have someone at the meeting who CAN make these decisions. My client will reject this IEP, and I'll initiate a hearing."

"Let's adjourn the meeting. I'll talk to my superiors and to Cognitive Kids about their opening. Don't initiate the hearing. I'll get back to you tomorrow."

"My clients and I need copies of your reports."

"Yes, we'll make copies right now."

After we received the copies of their reports, a copy of the proposed IEP, and the signature sheet, we all said our goodbyes. The IEP was merely the early intervention plan on a different form. The reports contained no useful information or recommendations. I figured if I didn't hear from Mary Carpenter the next day, I'd reject the IEP as Leila suggested.

When we were out the door, Leila said she'd walk us to our car. She looked behind to see if there was anyone else around. "They don't have a leg to stand on. None of those professionals are willing to put in writing that one hour a week is enough. You're the only one with the right pieces of paper. Their case will never hold up in a due process hearing. They'll probably get Cognitive Kids to write an IEP, and then you'll have another meeting. It's unlikely they'll continue to fight this. Many parents would have just taken the five months delay in service. It was worth their while to see if they could get you to agree. If this ended up at a hearing, it would look bad for the school district. They can get a reputation for fooling around like this. The hearing officer could become biased against them at the next case. It's probably good I came to the meeting. I believe everything will be fine in the end. Don't worry."

Of course, I had to be worried. I always thought that people went into special education to help disabled children. None of those folks stuck up for Abie. But then again, they must have refused to recommend the one-hour a week service in their reports.

Mary Carpenter called the next day. She scheduled another team meeting at Cognitive Kids. Much to our delight, she announced Abie would be starting Cognitive Kids the day after his third birthday.

Years later, I learned that IDEA requires school districts to write the IEP at the team meeting alongside the parents. According to the law, the parents are supposed to be included on the IEP team. Schools are not supposed to write IEPs and then present a *fait accompli* to the parents. They may write a draft, but they MUST be willing to accept parental input according to our federal and state laws.

While trying to prevent parental input in the process was and still is common practice, it is illegal. Many parents don't know this. I didn't know this in Abie's early years at school. Later on in Abie's school career, I did know this, but the schools had other ways of leveraging their power to make these decisions without parental input.

During the first week of school, I dropped Abie off at Cognitive Kids. Door-to-door transportation for Abie was to start the second week of school. They were going to pick him up at 8 am. When the first day of transportation finally arrived, I got him ready and I watched through the window for the van to arrive. At 8:30 am, I called the transportation company. The dispatcher told me the driver was on his way. We waited until 9 am. Still no van came. I called again. She said they were running a little late. They would arrive shortly. We waited again until 9:30 am, and then I called again. The dispatcher said the driver was stuck in a traffic jam. At that point, I said I'd drive him. At 3:30 pm, I received a call from Cognitive Kids.

No van had arrived to take him home. I got into my car, picked him up, and drove him home. Then I called the woman in charge of transportation for the district to tell her what happened. She assured me this was unusual. It wouldn't happen again. However, it happened again for the entire week and then off and on for years.

It was hard enough to send a vulnerable 3-year old child on a van by himself with strangers, but knowing I couldn't trust the drivers or the bus company made everything much worse.

I called the woman in charge of transportation for the school many times.

"It can take a while until all the schedules work out. You'll just have to be patient," she said.

"Abie is entitled to transportation according to his IEP."

"Yes, he's getting transportation, but it may take a while to get it going."

Transportation was always an issue that did improve somewhat at times, but we never straightened this out completely. Jon tried to fix this, but never made any headway. We always had problems.

Abie's Thoughts

One day Mommy took me to see a nasty woman. I didn't know she was actually a woman. I was little, so I saw her legs, which had blue pants on them, but I didn't see a face or anything at all past her waist. She looked just like a pair of walking legs. She smelled like the biggest smell in the world. It made my head hurt. Her pants were made of many threads woven together. Back then, I didn't know that threads were called "threads." The threads made many straight lines. Then those straight lines crossed other straight lines. I saw too many lines walking fast. As the legs walked, the bad smell went into my nose. Then the smell and the lines swooshed back and forth. I wanted to get away from those walking legs and that smell. The walking legs took me into a room away from Mommy. The walking legs didn't let me go to see if I would run after Mommy like Dr. Smith did. Instead, those scary legs sat me at a table across from them. Then I saw the legs had a face. It was a mean and scary face. I couldn't look at it. I wondered, "What is she going to do to me? How badly would it hurt? Would it be even worse than smelling that smell?"

I screamed. There were just the two of us in the room. She tried to get me to do some things. I had no interest. I cried a little, and then I tried to bite her. I tried to block her and everything else by waving and flapping my hands in front of my eyes. She called me a "retard" and said I was "uneducable."Then she said something that sounded like, "a waste of the taxpayers' money." That was the first time I heard the word, "retard," but I didn't know what it meant. I could feel that it was bad though. I felt this even though I didn't know words had any meaning. They were just sounds to me. I had heard many sounds back then like "reeetard." Reetard.. reetard.. Captain Peecard…Mommy's too fat to wear a leetard.

I knew the woman was especially mean by the way she dragged me in and out of the room, pulling my hand and arm and dragging me. I didn't want to go anywhere with her. I was very happy when I finally saw she was taking me back out to Mommy. I didn't look at Mommy, smile, or do anything to show I was glad…. but I was happier than ever to get away from those walking legs. Even though I was happy to see Mommy, I was mad at her too. Why would she make me go with those mean walking legs? I bit her hard when she helped me into the car. Then I pulled her hair and some of it actually came out.

When I was 3 years old, I went to school at Cognitive Kids all day long. A mean lady in a van came to pick me up. She was always late, and sometimes she didn't show up at all. I was scared to sit with her in the van. Sometimes she pulled the car off the road and hit me.

She hit me and hit me again, but I didn't know why. Then she yelled at me. When it was over, she went back on the road and drove to school or back home.

I saw Elsa twice a week at Cognitive Kids, but I spent most of my time in a classroom. I had a teacher named Candy. I wonder if she got that name from eating a lot of candy. It's possible she had some chocolate candy, but she was white. However, there were a few chocolate kids in my class, so maybe she gave the chocolate candy to them instead of me. Some real people and retards ate so much chocolate that their skin turned brown instead of white. They sure were lucky to have so much chocolate candy to eat! Chocolate people have very stimmy hair. I love to touch that hair. It's very soft. However, real people didn't want me to touch the hair and stim on it. I wonder why.

Leena was a chocolate retard in my class, and had chocolate people hair. She had twelve braids all over her head. Mommy said Leena looked cute in her *Polly Flinders* dresses. Someone cared about her and made her pretty. When Mommy said that, tears filled her eyes. I wanted to flip Leena's braids all day long, but Candy wouldn't let me flip Leena's braids at all. If Mommy saw me doing that, she took my hands away from them, and said, "No. Leave Leena alone." Nobody wanted me to have fun.

Anyway, Candy was white and pink and didn't have that type of hair. Instead, she had fluffy blond curls and dressed in outfits with no wrinkles in them. Real white people and chocolate people said she looked like a million bucks. She never looked like money to me. Money is green paper people use to buy stuff. The green wicked witch looked more like a million bucks than Candy did. Speaking of money, Daddy's job was to make money. It's possible he drew the money with green pencils, or perhaps he copied money on a Xerox machine. Back then, they had mimeograph machines. Maybe that was how he made the money. Anyway, Candy never looked like money even though the real people said she did. At the end of the school day, Candy's forehead was wet, her curls were uncurled, limp, and greasy, and her clothes were messy. Nobody ever said she looked like a million bucks at the end of the day…. only at the beginning of the day.

Candy followed Dr. Smith's orders. His orders were to get my class signing as soon as possible. We needed to sign, "give" every time we wanted something. Candy and her helpers, Jimmy and Louise, found all sorts of wonderful toys for all us retards. Some of us would line up the toys; some would bang them against the ground. I loved to wave them in front of my face while I made sounds or screamed. Mommy called the toys, "stimmers." "Stimmers" is autism talk for doing odd things over and over again for no particular purpose. Candy taught us to sign, "give" every time we wanted a stimmer or some food. Mommy saw Candy doing this, so she also made me sign, "give" every time I wanted something. Everyone was happy because my classmates and I were signing.

I could sign "give," but I didn't know everything in the world had its own name. I thought everything in the world had only one name, which was "give." Now I know this is wrong, but back then, I had no idea.

Then they tried to teach me another sign, "open." "Open" was when I needed help to get something out of something else. For example, I wanted a piece of candy, but if it was wrapped, I'd sign "open." Quickly I had two signs. When they tried to teach me a third sign, I had no use for it. Why would I need another sign? Didn't "give" and "open" cover everything?

Dr. Smith wanted me to find my jacket in a pile of jackets that belonged to other children. I couldn't do this task. It involved looking at too many things. It made me confused and unhappy. When I looked at the jackets, I saw zippers, snaps, elastic cuffs, and millions of threads. I also smelled the jackets. Some smelled like Tide with bleach alternative, and others just smelled like sweat, pizza, or spoiled ice cream. One of the jackets smelled like poop. I saw the colors flashing in my eyes from the jackets and coats....blue, black, red, green, and gray. I stood there and cried each time they wanted me to find my jacket. Also, they didn't give me stimmers or crackers or anything for finding my jacket. They expected me to understand the overwhelming world of different types of smelly jackets for no reason.

Many years later, Mommy said the jacket finding skill would have been a good thing for me to learn. I often lose my jacket or find myself wearing someone else's jacket.

After a while, Mommy said I had a plateau at Cognitive Kids. Plateau means I stopped learning. She said I needed to learn to be potty trained. Potty trained was very important to her, but Dr. Smith and Candy said I wasn't ready yet. Mommy was mad at Dr. Smith for not giving me food rewards or stimmers to help me learn other skills. She said his toolbox was limited. She was wrong. I never saw him with a toolbox at all. He had a briefcase, but it had papers in it. Not tools like hammers and wrenches.

Mommy needed "hope." Her hope stopped after I spent a year at Cognitive Kids. She said it was time for me to move on. One day I was in a new school, and I never saw Candy, Elsa, or Dr. Smith ever again.

Chapter 3: In Search of Medical Care

Arlene's Thoughts

The pediatrician missed the diagnosis when it was staring him in the face. His ignorance cheated Abie out of vital early intervention that could have made a difference in this life. He probably should have been sued, but I didn't want to sue him. I had too much work to do to get Abie on track. At the very least, he deserved to lose Abie as a patient. I was going to give our business to a better doctor, one who really deserved to earn money off us. After all, there were many pediatricians in the Newtucktin area. In my mind, it was just a matter of finding the best doctor.

Jayne Johnson recommended a pediatrician named Dr. Jones. She was the first pediatrician I called. The office manager answered the phone after three rings. That was a good sign.

"I'm looking for a new pediatrician for my three year old son. Is Dr. Jones taking on new patients?"

"Yes, she certainly is. Would you like me to send you some paperwork and information on our practice?" The office manager answered cheerfully.

"Yes, I'd like that, but there's something I need to tell you about my son. He's been diagnosed with autism. The doctor should be aware of that."

There was a pregnant pause. The silence was deafening. Something was wrong. Maybe I shouldn't have been so forthcoming with the information.

"We have five autism kids in the practice already. I don't know if we have the capacity to take on another one. I'm going to have to put you on hold while I find out some more information."

I was on hold for a full twenty minutes. I knew this wasn't going to be what I'd hoped for, but I stayed on the line anyway. I tried to lose myself in the *Muzak*. I didn't want to hear what I thought was coming next. As I waited, I shuddered at the thought that Dr. Jones might not be the only pediatrician who was hesitant to take on a kid like Abie. Perhaps the office manager hoped I would hang up. Eventually she came back to the phone. Maybe she wasn't going to reject us after all.

"Sorry to leave you on hold for so long. I'm sorry to say Dr. Jones is actually full, and cannot take on your son as a patient right now."

"What about the other doctors in the practice? Are any of them taking on new patients?"

"No, not at the moment, but we could put your son's name on our wait list."

"No, thanks." Abie's name would never come up on that wait list. There was no sense in pretending.

I called a few more pediatricians who were "full." A few practices openly admitted they didn't have the skills to handle a patient with autism.

Then I finally found Dr. Glenby. She sounded wonderful! Like a gift from heaven. She spoke to us directly. She was interested in helping Abie, and wanted to do everything she could to increase her knowledge of autism. She even offered to attend an IEP meeting. Unfortunately, Dr. Glenby was not on our managed care insurance plan. I was devastated.

I called the insurance, and explained our problem. I thought, "Perhaps they'd make an exception, and allow us to use an out of network pediatrician." I hoped and prayed to no avail. Instead, they assured me there were many pediatricians in my area taking on new patients. They suggested I call back some of the practices that had previously rejected Abie. It was no use. There was nobody our insurance covered who was willing to take Abie on as a patient. I was stuck.

Then I received a letter. Abie's current pediatrician, the one I wanted to fire, was retiring. A new pediatrician was taking his place. We were already in that practice, so there was no way they could reject us. Since I had no choice, I figured we'd give Dr. Williams a chance.

Dr. Williams had no clue about autism, and didn't know what to do about Abie. He couldn't examine him, calm him, give us advice or resources concerning autism, or do anything else a pediatrician might do. He treated Abie like an inanimate object, and never spoke directly to him. But he was a pediatrician, and we needed somebody.

Abie appeared to be frequently in pain with what we thought was constant ear infections. However, who could really tell? Dr. Williams had difficulty examining his ears. Abie would flail about and try to bite when we held him still. He also cried and screamed. An ear can turn bright red from crying and screaming.

His eardrum burst occasionally. Blood and pus oozed out. We knew something was going on in that area. Sometimes when we took him to Dr. Williams, he could have had an ear infection, and sometimes it might have been something else. Nobody knew for sure.

Dr. Williams prescribed antibiotics that didn't work, and then he prescribed stronger antibiotics that had side effects like diarrhea....and sometimes those didn't work either.

He referred Abie to an ear, nose, and throat specialist, otherwise known as an ENT. It was difficult to get an appointment with the specialist. So we still visited Dr. Williams for the frequent ear infections, but the specialist did help us.

Abie saw the specialist every six months. This was like a visit to hell. Actually, maybe it wasn't like hell. Is there some place a little worse than hell? That was what it was like. Sometimes the doctor left us waiting in the waiting room for over two hours. I brought a wide variety of toys Abie could stim on, and a huge bag of snacks and goodies. I prayed my stash would last until the doctor finally saw him. The longer the wait, the less likely Abie would cooperate with the doctor's examination.

Abie made stimmy noises in the waiting room. Some of the noises were loud and sounded like screaming. The parents of the normal children complained that he was disturbing them and their children. I wondered what they thought I could do to remedy the situation. I tried my hardest to distract Abie, so the stim noises would subside a little. If I gave him food, he couldn't make noises with all of the chewing and swallowing he had to do. When I did that, the receptionist gave me a dirty look. "Food is not allowed in the waiting area. I'll make an exception this time if you clean up afterwards. This area MUST be spotless!"

I groveled and thanked the receptionist profusely for this meager accommodation. I was learning my place as a special needs mother. Grovel and thank.

Once when Abie was having a hard time, I asked the receptionist if the doctor could see us next.

"There are a few patients here who have appointments before yours. We have to take them first," she said.

"But we were here before the other patients showed up, and my son is disabled and can't wait."

"All young children have difficulty waiting. You have to wait your turn like everyone else. The doctor is behind because of an emergency."

There was always an emergency in that office, and we weren't anything like everyone else waiting in that office.

Eventually the ENT recommended ear tubes for Abie. That helped. By the time Abie's ear problems subsided at age twelve, the ENT was recommending eardrops instead of antibiotics, and there was more awareness of the overuse of antibiotics.

Some of the other parents at Cognitive Kids recommended a pediatrician's office affiliated with a big hospital. They were willing to take Abie on as a patient. They also had nurses available to help us with getting Abie to cooperate. They limited all our appointments to fifteen minutes or less, but it was a better experience overall. Fifteen minutes was probably what our insurance allowed, but it never seemed to be a reasonable allotment for a child with complex needs.

Abie's Thoughts

I hated being sick. First one side of your nose doesn't work, then the other side of your nose doesn't work, then your ear and throat gets stopped up with invisible knives, pokers, and stabbers that stab in and out. Mommy was so stupid. I felt bad enough as it was with being sick. To make me feel even worse, she brought me to a doctor who was interested in stabbing something into the very spot where I felt the worst. This made no sense at all. It hurt in my ear. I didn't want anyone to touch me there. But that was nothing compared to what came next.

After almost every visit with that horrible doctor, I ended up seeing sicky sweet pink liquid in our refrigerator. When I saw that, I tried to pour it out, but it wouldn't pour. Then Mommy quickly took it away from me. She wanted me to drink that stuff from a spoon. Yucky! I hated that stuff. It smelled like the stuff people put in their mouths when they chew a pink bubble-making thing that pops.

When they chew that stuff, they spit it out. They never swallow it. You know why? Because it tastes worse than the biggest smell in the world. So I made up my mind. There was no way I was going to drink that awful pink stuff.

Mommy tried to force the spoon in my mouth. I wasn't having it. I spit it right into her face. I saw the pink stuff squirt into her face, hair, and clothing. Awful smelling pink dots were all over the place. That was the good part. I thought the pink spray would end the problem, but Mommy had other ideas.

She had a squirty thing called a syringe. She filled it up with that pink stuff. Then she held my nose and squirted it in the back of my throat. When she let go of my nose, I felt like either I had to swallow the pink stuff or I was going to choke. So I swallowed it. I tried everything I could to get away from Mommy when she had that syringe squirter filled with that pink stuff. But I was little and she was big. She could run faster than me. She could make me still to hold my nose and squirt that in. Why would Mommy do such a thing?

Sometimes the pink stuff would disappear from the refrigerator. Oh boy, was I glad! Then a bottle with banana smelling stuff would appear in the refrigerator in the same spot. The banana smelling stuff had a taste even worse than the pink stuff. Every time Mommy made me drink the banana stuff, I would poop liquidy poop all day long until my tushy was sore. So not only did I have an ear that hurt, I also had a rear that hurt.

One day Mommy gave me nothing to eat even though I was hungry. Then I went to the hospital. Anytime anyone mentions a hospital, it's time to panic. A hospital is a bad place. In the hospital, people in costumes poke you, stick you with needles, and make you dress in ridiculous clothes with no underwear. If you can figure out a way to get out of there, you're lucky. I tried to run, but since I was only four years old, the grownups caught me. Anyway, I fell asleep there, and while I fell asleep, they put tubes in my ears. After that, my ears hurt less.

Chapter 4: Happily Ever After

Jon's Thoughts

I always thought being married would be wonderful. "Married" meant you never ever had to be lonely because you had a partner in life, a helper in life. But sometimes I do feel lonely. "Married" also meant you got many other goodies like love and attention. After people get married in fairy tales, they always lived happily ever after, but fairy tales aren't anything like real life. In fairy tales, nobody has to deal with autism, the special education system, the healthcare system, or the Department of Mental Retardation.

I remember looking at a picture of Arlene and me with Abie. We were so happy. After the diagnosis, I began to wonder if we would ever be happy like that again. Would we ever smile? Would we always feel like we were sinking into an abyss?

When Abie was young, I remember thinking about how other families brought their kids to a park to play, and their kids knew exactly how to play. Other families bought toys for their kids, and just like a miracle, they played with those toys appropriately. Then those very same parents had the audacity to complain that their children begged them for more and more toys. Most parents don't know how lucky they are. How I wished Abie begged for toys!

If Abie wasn't stimming, his behavior was destructive. Kick a wall in. Bite my arm. He wasn't interested in much of anything. This wasn't the family life I wanted.

Arlene was always so mad at me. I didn't know how to engage Abie in anything. She was so much better at it than I was. I just let her take the responsibility for doing it. From time to time, I did try to help. She had trouble with Abie's transportation. I tried talking to them. I tried straightening it out...really I did. That transportation woman was really something. I never spoke to someone who cared so little about doing her job well. Anyway, I lost it, and maybe made matters worse. I offered to take care of Abie while Arlene went to a support group. My heart was in my stomach for the whole time she was gone. I just prayed I would be able to get by until she came home.

When I came home for work, she begged me to spend some time with Abie so she could have a break. I had no idea of how to do this. I didn't know how to raise an autistic son. Why did this happen to us?

I never wanted to spend time doing things I don't do well. Arlene couldn't work because no daycare would take someone like Abie. I was the breadwinner. I made good money as a software engineer. So my mission was to do well with that. I focused on work. I worked long days and had a long commute. I left for work at 7 am and when I came home at 8 pm, I was tired. I was a good steady provider for my family. I couldn't deal much with helping out. Arlene constantly talked about Abie's intervention. It was as if she was possessed. Where was the woman I married? Her life was all about helping him. Can't say as I blamed her. We couldn't rely on the professionals. She was Abie's only hope. No wonder parents of kids with autism get divorced and die young. We won't get divorced, though. We're in it for the long haul.

.

Chapter 5: A New School

I had an appointment to visit the Behavioral School at 9 am sharp. I was as nervous as can be. Places like the Behavioral School demanded a loyal following. I learned this at my support group. A loyal following means you believe the chosen school is the best there is. You don't question their expertise...EVER. I chose Cognitive Kids instead of the Behavioral School in the first place. That was a count against me.

Patricia Stone, the director of the school, met me at the door and explained how the school worked. "We're an applied behavior analysis school. Unlike Cognitive Kids, the methodology used at the Behavioral School has a scientific basis. We also boast an outstanding award-winning home program. Studies have shown that children with autism benefit from exposure to neurotypical peers. "Neurotypical" is the term we use for children who are developing normally. We use this term instead of the term "normal" because it IS normal for some children to have atypical development. Because children like Abie benefit from being with neurotypical peers, we have an integrated preschool program. We haven't yet found a way to integrate our school age program, but we're looking into the possibility. Our program is so effective that we return many of our students back to their home districts. Our program is very intense.... thirty hours of rigorous behavioral teaching, and most of it is one-on-one."

First, my heart soared at the prospect of Abie finally getting the help he needed, then my heart sank because I should have chosen the Behavioral School in the first place. Cognitive Kids wasn't really thirty hours a week of intervention. They had trouble engaging the students for that amount of time. There was significant down time. I questioned my previous decisions, "Why didn't I change Abie's school sooner? Why didn't I give him the chance to be in an innovative integrated preschool where he could receive intensive intervention? "

Patricia led me through the hall and opened a door. There I saw what looked like a preschool for normal kids. There were crayon drawings on the wall with golden star stickers I remembered from my own childhood. Toys were neatly stored away. Everything was organized perfectly, and everyone was appropriately engaged. I saw kids playing, drawing, and doing a group activity. I didn't see any self-stimulatory behavior…no flapping, shaking, making funny noises, or running back and forth. I said, "I can't tell which students are the ones with autism and which are the neurotypical peers."

"Thank you. That's because we've done our jobs exceptionally well. Of course, I can't tell you which children carry a diagnosis because of privacy laws. See how ALL of the children are following directions."

"I can't picture my Abie following along like that in a classroom like that."

Patricia smiled confidently. "We work with many children like your son. Some of them aren't ready for an integrated situation right away, but after a short time of working with us, they ARE ready. Let's go to my office, and we can talk about your son."

We walked down a long hallway with many closed doors. "Do those doors lead to other classrooms?"

"Yes, we have some other classrooms, and we have a few quiet rooms students use when they are overwhelmed and need a calming place. I would show you the other classrooms, but I don't want to disturb the intense learning. Please step this way." She led me into a very nice large office with a conference table on the side. We took our seats at either side of the conference table.

Patricia took out the copy of Abie's IEP and frowned. "Cognitive Kids writes a very strange IEP. We wouldn't be able to honor this. We'll have to write a completely new IEP."

"That's fine. I thought you would probably say that."

"So why have you decided to change your son's placement?"

"I'm not seeing the progress I was hoping for. I want to work on toilet training with Abie. He just turned four years old. Cognitive Kids says he's not ready to start potty training. Also, I want to work on oral speech before he turns five."

"Why didn't you choose the Behavioral School in the first place?"

"Patricia, I assure you …I'm fully committed to this program. I'm very impressed. It would be so wonderful if Abie had the opportunity to attend here."

"Mrs. Dancer, we'll be happy to work on what concerns you if we decide to admit Abie. We work with parents as a team. We also have a four to six month home-based program. This program will help your son generalize the skills he learns here to the environment at home. Would you be willing to work with one of our therapists in your home?"

"WOULD I?" I answered excitedly, "That sounds wonderful! Like a dream come true! Do you have an opening?"

"We'll have to test Abie, and see if he is appropriate for our program. We don't have an opening just yet, but we might have one in a few weeks. We have many children on our wait list. We'll be selecting the students and the families who fit best with our programming. We can't promise anything, but we'll do our best. In the meantime, please discuss your desire to switch placements with your school district. We wouldn't be able to accept Abie if your district doesn't fund the placement."

"I have to tell you something else. Abie's developed a self-stimulatory behavior I would really like to get rid of."

"What's the behavior?"

"Abie's discovered saliva. He continuously takes spit out of his mouth, slaps it on a table, a wall, the floor, or any place. Then he swirls his finger around in the saliva. I'm constantly cleaning this up. He does this all over my house. He's obsessed with doing this."

"We're experts in extinguishing or reducing behaviors such as you describe. We'll be certain to address this behavior if he's accepted. Do you have any further questions?"

"No, I think you've covered everything. I'll call Mary Carpenter from the school district and tell her about my desire to switch Abie."

I squirmed in my seat as I thought about the possibility that they might not admit Abie. It was time for grovel, thank, and beg. "Thank you so much for meeting with me today. I'm so very impressed by you and by the program. Please accept Abie into this program. He got off to a rough start with his intervention. He really didn't get the early intervention he should have. Then I made the mistake of choosing Cognitive Kids. A placement here at the Behavioral School is going to make a huge difference in his life. Thank you so much for considering him."

"We'll do our best, but we can't guarantee Abie placement."

As soon as I arrived home, I called Mary Carpenter. "Mary, I want to thank you for all of your help in the past, but there's something I need to discuss with you. I'm concerned with Abie's progress at Cognitive Kids, and I'm looking into a placement at the Behavioral School. Right now, I'm not sure they'll accept him. But if they do, I'm hoping the district would support this move. "

"I'm not sure how to do the paperwork to move him from one private placement to another. It's very unusual for parents to make such a move. Most are just thrilled to pieces just to get the private placement. After all, private placements are very costly for the school district. These costs take away from the education of typical students. A move may involve some extensive paperwork on my part. I'm too busy now to consider this for him."

"Abie needs to get potty trained, and his oral speech is not progressing." I was too embarrassed to tell Mary Carpenter that the program I chose never worked on oral speech at all. I wondered whether the school district might have a placement for Abie. It would be an advantage to have him close to home. "If you have a specialty autism classroom within the district, I'd be willing to consider that."

Mary hesitated for a minute. "We don't have a place for Abie within the district. Once we get over the paperwork hurdle, the costs to the school district are the same whether he attends Cognitive Kids or the Behavioral School. So on second thought, we might support the move if you're certain this is what you want. "

"Yes, I want this for Abie if they'll accept him." I wondered why Mary changed her mind all of a sudden. According to the law, the district must consider a placement within the school district first before placing a student out of district. She didn't want to consider bringing him into the district. Perhaps this had something to do with Mary's sudden change of heart.

"Okay. I'll call them, and see if I can facilitate this. You should know, however, that uprooting a child from a placement carries a consequence. You should be positive you really want this before you uproot him. My advice as a professional with many years' experience in the field is to keep him at Cognitive Kids."

Mary's advice couldn't sway me one way or another. I already believed she had her own agenda.

"Please go ahead and talk to the Behavioral School. Their program is much more suited to Abie. I also want to thank you again for all of your help... this time and in the past. I appreciate your support."

A month later, the Behavioral School accepted Abie into their program. Patricia called to say her team thought he wasn't ready for the integrated setting, but he would be perfect for another classroom. She invited me to come back and observe the other classroom before Jon and I made our final decision.

The classroom they were proposing for Abie was quite different from the integrated classroom. There were no typical peers, and there was flapping, stim noises, crying, and tantrums in the room. However, there were only six children in the classroom and three teachers. They were doing discrete trial teaching when we observed. Discrete trial teaching is intensive teaching using the principles of applied behavior analysis otherwise known as ABA. This method helps with skill acquisition and reduction of maladaptive behavior. Children sat at tables, and teachers gave them rewards for completing certain tasks. The rewards were salty chips, candies, and cookies, and toys that a child like Abie might use for self-stimulatory behavior.

It was odd to see food rewards used freely in this program. I used food rewards at home, but I kept that a secret. The staff at Cognitive Kids was quite adamant… food rewards were not good for children…any children. The children I saw were learning to imitate, to follow directions, and other important skills. The imitation was a simple "do this" action with body parts, and the directions were commands like, "sit down, stand up, clap your hands, etc."

In general, the classroom looked good to me, but certainly not as good as the integrated classroom. Patricia assured me they would work on oral speech and on toilet training. I was fine with having him in a substantially separate classroom for a while. They were going to do so much for him. So I would have to wait a little while for him to get to the integrated classroom. It was no big deal. They admitted Abie to the school on a three-month diagnostic placement. After the three months, they would know him better and be ready to write an IEP.

I was particularly interested in the imitation programs. Imitation seemed like an essential skill. Once a person imitated, he would be able to use that skill to learn many other skills.

After the three-month diagnostic placement was up, I received a call from Abie's case worker, Jenny. She arranged for the two of us to meet to discuss the upcoming IEP. She presented possible goals and objectives. For the oral speech program, he was to imitate three sounds: "B" "K" and "D." He was going to work on following one-step instructions, match pictures to objects, receptive pointing to three objects: cup, fork, and napkin, do a simple puzzle and a shape box, build a block tower and a train, produce eye contact on demand, produce appropriate greetings, and wash his hands.

They were also going to work on having him point to pictures on a communication board. I wasn't too sure about his picture recognition, but I didn't want to argue… so I went along with that. The behavior plan included working on his spit stimming and out-of-seat behaviors. They were also going to address toilet training goals in the home program.

I was elated by the goals on the proposed IEP, but Jenny didn't mention imitation. When I asked about it, she told me they tested his imitation. He did it perfectly for three staff members. They showed me the raw baseline data. I was totally shocked. I had tried to do this with him, and he didn't do it. The only time he ever did the imitation was when they tested him. They were very accommodating and happy to add this to his education plan. Things were definitely looking up. He was four years old…under that magic age of five. He could still beat the odds and have a normal life.

I was absolutely in heaven at the thought of not having to hide the fact that I used a system of rewards, including food rewards, to help Abie learn. At last, I could be honest and open. I could work as a team with his teachers…..or so I thought.

Abie's Thoughts

When I was four, I noticed real people said the same things over and over again, and a certain thing was connected to what they said. For instance, if Mommy said we were going to the doctor, I always ended up in a place where a nasty big person would poke me and do nasty things. Even though I noticed this, I still didn't know everything in the world had its own name.

One day Mommy took me to a new place where many white ladies tried to get me to do things. These ladies had cheese curls, popcorn, crackers, M & M's, and Skittles there. They also had many stimmers such as two soda bottles connected together with water in it. They called it "the tornado." They had rubber snakes, koosh balls, bouncy balls, and slimy clay called "gak." All the stimmers were great for blocking out bad things, but there was a catch. If you wanted to get a stimmer, you had to do all sorts of things that made no sense at all.

First, Mommy took me there for a few hours one afternoon. She called this, "an evaluation." Then one day, instead of going to my regular school, Mommy took me to that place. I went there every weekday instead of going to Cognitive Kids. Everything was different there. I didn't want to be there even though they had those nice stimmers. However, I was four years old, so I had no choice.

When I got upset about being there, they put me in the quiet room. Sometimes they called it the time-out room. Other times they called it "the jail." It was a special jail for PDD low-functioning uneducable autistic retards. It was a closet-size room with nothing in it, no windows, but it had a door. I had to go to the quiet room many times. I signed "give" to get the stimmers and the food, but the white ladies who they called "teachers" just ignored me. Then I got mad and had a tantrum. Their sets of rules were different from Mommy's rules or the rules in my old school. This made me upset and angry, so I had to go to the jail for PDD low functioning uneducable autistic retards.

When I tried to get out of my seat, the hand of the teacher, Jenny, pushed my head down from the back of my neck. Sometimes my head would hit the desk when she did that, and it would hurt. I didn't want Jenny's hands to touch me. At Cognitive Kids, they touched you to hug you, tickle you, or kiss you. I didn't like the kissing and hugging at first, but after a while I actually liked it. I don't think I would ever like the way Jenny's hands grabbed me and took me to the jail, or the way she and some of the other teachers would grab the back of my neck and force my head down on a desk.

When I was at Cognitive Kids, Candy called my name, then I came, and she swung me. I liked that. Candy called that "following directions." In my new school, "following directions" meant something different. The teacher told me to stand up. If I stood up, I'd get a food reward or a stimmer. But then, for no reason at all, she told me to sit down. I might also get a reward for sitting down, but why did the teacher ask me to stand up when she wanted me to sit down? I was sitting down in the first place.

The teacher asked me to point to a cup. She held her hand over my hand and made me point to a cup. I got a reward for that. Then she asked me to point to something I never heard of called "a napkin." Well, since pointing to the cup did the trick that last time, I just did it again. So then, she grabbed my hand and made me point to the other thing, the napkin. She said, "This is pointing to napkin." I hated doing this. The teachers made me to do this over and over again. I tried to block them out by stimming.

After a while, I did learn the words "cup, fork, and napkin" but I never really paid attention to the pointing part, so it took a while before I could prove I knew it. Proving you know it is more important to the grown up real people than actually knowing something. Even though I learned the words "cup," "fork," and "napkin," I still didn't yet know that each and everything in the world had its own name, and I didn't know words could be used for asking for things, naming things, and explaining things.

When I first arrived in the new place, the teachers did something they called a "baseline evaluation." They made me do all sorts of things, but I didn't get the food rewards or the stimmer rewards for doing what they wanted. However, I didn't know this was the deal. I thought I was going to get some good rewards. I saw other kids getting rewards, so I assumed I would too. I was able to concentrate hard and imitate. When Mommy asked me to imitate, I didn't want to do it. What would I get for doing it? Just a cracker. It wasn't worth it just for a measly cracker. The imitation was hard for me, so I needed a very powerful reward in order to do it correctly.

I stopped signing "give" so much. Mommy spoke to my teachers about it. They told her they would honor my signing. They didn't believe in signing because the staff in adult services doesn't understand signing. The staff in adult services might have caught PDD low-functioning uneducable retard autism too. After all, how difficult is it to understand two signs? Unfortunately, despite Mommy's efforts, my teachers continued to ignore my signing. When my signing had practically disappeared, she tried to get me to point instead of signing "give." The pointing actually worked with the teachers sometimes. Pointing confused me. Mommy wanted me to point because I wanted something, and my teachers wanted me to point to things that I didn't want....such as cup, fork, and napkin. Pointing had to do with something they called "joint attention." Some teachers did joint attention with some weeds at a party. I heard them talking about that.

Life became overwhelming in the new school. I tried to get out of my seat and escape. When I did that, the teachers would force my head down and make me go back to my seat. My teachers were just clothes and body parts. I didn't see them as total human beings the way I saw Mommy or Elsa. They were a hand, pieces of a face, a voice, or legs walking. I couldn't put them together to make sense of them. I couldn't look at them even though they gave me stimmers and cheese curls. They were not my friends.

My day at school started with circle time. Circle time was almost the same as at Cognitive Kids so I liked it. At circle time, the teachers told you what the date was and what the day of the week was. Then we sang songs, but not the way Mommy sang songs with me. When she sang with me, she stopped in the middle of the song and I would finish it. She always wanted me to sing the last word. I had a strong urge to finish the last word of the song most of the time. I wanted the song to finish the right way.

There was something I liked to do over and over again to make myself feel better. I make stuff in my mouth called "spit." Anyway, I made as much of it as I wanted. I never seemed to run out of it. I made this stuff all by myself. I used the spit to make a little puddle on a chair or table or any surface. Then I swirled my finger around the spit. I blocked out all annoyances by concentrating on doing this. My teachers gave me little pieces of cheese curls every five minutes for not doing this. I preferred to swirl my spit than get those pieces of cheese curls even though cheese curls were delicious. Then the teachers started giving me cheese curls every two minutes for not doing the spit swirls. That was a deal too good to pass up. Eventually I forgot about how good it felt to do spit swirls. Instead, I liked to find an object such as a spoon or other hard utensil, and I banged it against a surface. Mommy didn't like this because I made little holes in her new furniture. She said life was better when I was doing the spit stims.

It was very important for me to imitate the sounds, "B," "K," and "D." I practiced this every day with Mommy before I went to school, when I came home, and every weekend until I did this perfectly. I had no idea why she wanted me to imitate those sounds. I didn't know that it had something to do with speaking or communicating.

I also worked with something called a "shape box." Mommy got mad at my teachers and Patricia, the boss, because I was able to fit a round circle into the square hole using the shape box they gave me at school. She told Jenny the materials were inappropriate. A few days after that, she sent me to school with a new shape box. When I came to school with the new shape box, Patricia and Jenny looked at it together. After a few minutes, Patricia said, "I guess the shape box we had wasn't good enough for Her Royal Highness."

Those teachers gave me a ball, a Frisbee, a cup and a fork. They also gave me pictures of those four objects. The objects were big, but the pictures were small. The objects looked nothing like the pictures.

"Match it, Abie," Jenny said. First, she put her hands over mine and placed an object on each of the pictures, and then they gave me an M& M. However, they wanted me to do this by myself, and I had no idea what to do. Once, Mommy saw me doing this at school. She told Jenny I needed an extra step to help me understand what I was supposed to do. They told Mommy she was smart to make that suggestion. They also thanked her many times. Then they just kept on doing it the way they always did it. I got frustrated because I didn't know what to do with the pictures and objects. I had tantrums because of that. Then I had to go to the quiet room jail for PDD uneducable low functioning autistic retards.

At home, Mommy got smaller objects and drew pictures of the objects on pieces of paper. The objects and the drawings were the same size. It took only a few times before I understood what I was supposed to do with matching those objects to the drawings. Then I understood what Jenny wanted me to do with their little pictures and the big objects. After that, I understood what pictures were, and I started to watch movies and videos. Mommy called this "a breakthrough." She was very happy I started to watch videos because I had no play behavior. I only had stimming behavior and what my teachers called, "maladaptive behavior." "Maladaptive behavior" are fancy words for doing all sorts of things like kicking the wall, emptying cabinets, and biting my wrist. I also liked to turn on the faucet, stick my finger under the tap, and watch the water fly all around the room. It was great, but Mommy didn't like it and wanted to stop me from doing it.

I also had other breakthroughs. When I was at Cognitive Kids, Elsa told Mommy that Maureen Pauley was the best babysitter for me. Maureen had long blond hair and big blue eyes. She was the most beautiful lady in the entire world. She worked at Cognitive Kids and the Behavioral School. At the Behavioral School, she worked in the integrated classroom, not in my classroom. Sometimes when she passed me in the hallway, she stooped down to my size, and said "hello there, Abie, my cutie."

One weekend, Mommy and Daddy went away to some place called a hotel. Who knows why they went there without me. What an odd thing to do. Anyway, they went to a hotel, and Maureen came to take care of me. She gathered many stimmers and little pieces of candy, cheese curls, and crackers. She also gathered together puzzles and many toys I didn't like because I never used them as stimmers. All weekend long, she offered me things. When she was about to give me something I liked, she took my head in her hands and made my head go up and down. Then she gave me what I wanted. When she was about to give me something I didn't want, she made my head turn from side to the other side… and then she didn't give me what I didn't want. We did this all weekend except for the times we slept. By the end of the weekend I nodded my head "yes" when I wanted something, and shook my head "no" when I didn't want something. When Mommy and Daddy came back from their weekend, Maureen told them she had a big surprise for them. Then we showed them how I was able to nod and shake my head for "yes" and "no." I don't think Mommy liked the surprise because she couldn't stop crying when she saw me do this. Mommy said this was also a breakthrough.

Chapter 6: On the Van

Arlene's Thoughts

Abie had two van mates on his trips to the Behavioral School. One was Danny and the other was Matt. Matt got picked up first. Then either Danny or Abie would get picked up depending on the traffic conditions. Coming home, Danny or Abie would be dropped off first, and then Matt would be dropped off. Matt lived the furthest away from the school.

I was used to seeing significantly delayed children. Danny seemed like a neurotypical child to me. While I buckled Abie in his car seat, Danny once told me he was going skiing that weekend. He also told me his mother is a behavioral psychologist. "My Daddy teaches really big kids who look like grownups in a school called a college. Not little kids like me." One day he handed me a piece of paper. "This is for you, Abie's mommy."

Abie's mom,

Please call me when you have a chance to talk. 888-6771.

Best,
Mandy Greenberg (Danny's mom).

It was difficult for parents of special needs children to make contact with the other parents outside of a few support groups. There were no PTAs in private special needs schools and family events were either rare or nonexistent. The schools refused to give out telephone numbers and names to parents who wanted to network. They always claimed they couldn't because of possible HIPAA violations. I believed the schools didn't want parents to be talking to each other, and they used HIPAA as an excuse. I was very happy Mandy Greenberg reached out to me.

I called Mandy. "This is Arlene Dancer, Abie's mom. I got your note."

"Oh! I'm so glad you called. I want to compare notes with you. I went to observe Danny the other day, and I saw Abie having a hard time. Did they call you?"

"No, they didn't. What do you mean by a hard time?"

"I think they put him into the jail."

A knot formed in my stomach. "What do you mean? The jail?"

"That's what some parents call the seclusion room."

My heart sank. I recalled Marilyn Taylor from early intervention telling me about the school using seclusion and restraint. Patricia Stone, the director of the school, never mentioned anything about that. "Oh wait!" I thought, "Maybe she did. She might have mentioned something about 'quiet rooms'."

I imagined Abie alone in a seclusion room. "Oh no."

"Listen, don't worry about one time in the time-out room. If it becomes a regular thing, then you have a problem. You just need to monitor it. It's important for us to talk to each other. When you go in to observe Abie, I want you to peek in at Danny if you can. I want to know what's going on. I'll do the same for you. We need to stick together."

"I don't know if I can see much. Danny's in a different classroom."

Mandy insisted. "Listen, they won't suspect a thing. Tell them you need to look in to learn from their expertise. Flattery is everything. Even if you don't peek in, you might know if Danny gets taken to the time-out room. I just want you to tell me if you happen to see something."

"They take kids from the integrated class and they put them in the jail?" I asked incredulously.

"Well, they put those kids in the jail less often than the non-verbal kids. The verbal kids, whether they're in the integrated class or not, can go home and tell their parents. The non-verbal kids can't."

"Would they ever put a typical child in there?"

"They could get into big trouble for doing that. No, probably not."

I thought for a moment. "The quiet room is scary, but if a kid is going wild and is hitting and damaging everything in sight, what alternative do they have?"

"What do you do when Abie has a tantrum?"

"I find a place for a time-out where he can do no damage. I let him tantrum it out as much as possible, but I wouldn't let him hurt himself. In a way, they're doing the same thing as I am."

"The difference is in the timing and supervision. Once he calms, I'll bet he gets out right away. I also think you're keeping tabs on him."

"I usually count to ten after he is calm. Then he comes out. "

"After a while he might learn to calm himself when he gets angry, and eventually the tantrum behavior might start to disappear. The staff at the school is supposed to receive training on proper procedure for time-out, but parents are never privy to the details of the trainings or the details regarding the time-out procedure. There's supposed to be some kind of incident report. They should send a copy to the parents, but they never do."

"They didn't do seclusion at Cognitive Kids, but on the other hand, Abie didn't make as much progress there as he has so far at the Behavioral School."

"Well, they each have their advantages. Maybe it's good Abie had a little of both. I'm a behavioral psychologist, but I brought Danny to Cognitive Kids for a few sessions. I thought it was helpful."

I couldn't believe my ears. "WOW, let me get this straight....you're a behaviorist..... AND you were open to another approach? It seems to me this doesn't happen too much."

"Yes, I know what you're talking about. Of course, it's different when it's your own kid."

"The school doesn't really listen to me. Since you're a behavioral psychologist, is it different for you?"

"I usually don't work with people with autism in my profession.... but of course, I don't say that to the people at the school. Some of them do listen to me and some don't. Most don't because regardless of what I do for a living, I'm still the mother. Speaking of staff working with the mothers, I wanted to ask you about Abie's home program. How's it going?"

"Abie's going to start the home program next week. I'm very excited and hopeful."

"The home program was very good for Danny. I wanted to do only the home program and forget about the school. There's too much down time at the school. He made much greater strides in the home program."

"Oh, the home program sounds wonderful. We're going to work on toilet training. What did you work on?"

"I toilet trained Danny a while back. We worked on language and social skills. We used my daughter as a typical peer model, and we did many social stories. It was great."

I felt a hint of envy. Abie seemed light years from practicing social skills. "You said there's a lot of downtime at the school. Whenever I observed, they were doing discrete trials."

"Yes, they always schedule visits so you see the discrete trials. Then they have naptime and lunch. The parents usually leave during naptime because that's boring. The staff encourages you to leave at that time, too. If you stay through naptime and lunch, you'll see there's another discrete trial session. It lasts an hour in the afternoon. Then the rest is free time."

"So you don't think our kids are getting thirty hours a week of intense intervention?"

"No, absolutely not. It's more like ten to fifteen hours a week of intervention. The rest is babysitting."

"Mandy, what was Danny like before he entered the integrated classroom? When did he learn to speak? When did he develop play behavior?"

"Danny developed language and play behavior while he was in early intervention. He received specialty services from the Behavioral School Home Programming Specialty Services for ten hours a week. That service was like the home program you are about to get. Danny was like he is now when he entered the school, but now he knows about taking turns and sharing, and is much more socially aware. He plays with a few typical peers."

"How often do kids from the self-contained classrooms graduate into the integrated classroom?"

"It does happen… but it happens very rarely. They accepted most of the students in the integrated classroom specifically for that classroom. Only one of them actually came from a self-contained classroom."

"Hmm. That is not exactly what they told me. Do you know how many kids get returned to their home districts after having been at the school?"

"Many leave for their home districts, but that doesn't mean they had a jump in learning. Most of the time they leave to go back to their home districts because the parents aren't satisfied. They want to try something else. Five students left the preschool programming around the time Abie came in. Four went back to their home districts and one went to Cognitive Kids."

It was upsetting to hear the truth, but in the deepest depths of my heart, I already knew what Mandy was telling me. "I'm so glad you called. I'm going to do my best to keep my eye on Danny. It's been so helpful to talk these things out. "

"I am glad I called too, but now I have to tell you the real reason I called. Matt's mother, Darlene, is trying to get him picked up last to go to school, and dropped off first. For our kids, it means backtracking, and it doesn't make any sense. The bus company might call you and talk to you about this. I'm angry about the situation, and I let them know that. This will bring our kids' commute to over an hour. By law, they can't do that. We need to have a united front on this."

"Wow, why would they even think about doing something like that? They'd have to pass our blocks and then go back to where they came from. It makes no sense."

"Well, apparently, Darlene spoke to the right people or perhaps she has connections. Anyway, a commute of over an hour is not legal. We need to both stick to that. Maybe they'll give Matt his own van."

"Do you think talking to Darlene might do something?"

"No, not at all. I already tried it."

"Okay then, what do I do?"

"We need to call Mary Carpenter on the same day and around the same time. Then, if they still decide to go according to Darlene's plan, we can call the Department of Education and complain that they are violating the one hour rule."

"I'm in. Let's see if they do it, then we can make plans to call."

The transportation company never called me to tell me they were going to change the drop-off and pick up schedule. They just went ahead and did it according to the way Darlene wanted it. When they started traveling a way Abie was unfamiliar with, he started screaming, crying, and flailing all about. In the end, I didn't have to fight the pickup and drop off schedule. Abie's tantrum straightened this out for us. However, this was the beginning of a long-term battle with the school system. Abie needed a bus monitor for his long trips back and forth to the school. The school district wasn't interested in paying for a bus monitor even if it meant the children and the driver's safety was at risk.

Danny Greenberg did well in the integrated classroom. The school district returned him to a regular kindergarten in Newtucktin. After kindergarten, his father received a career opportunity in New York. Mandy called me after their move to New York, but I never reciprocated. It was hard to hear about Danny's progress. In comparison, Abie's gains were puny. Many years later, I felt sad I hadn't kept in touch with Mandy Greenberg, a person who tried to help us. I once reached out to her on LinkedIn, but she never replied. Perhaps she didn't remember who I was. I never found out if Danny Greenberg was one of the lucky ones to live a mainstream life after having a diagnosis of autism.

Abie's Thoughts

One day the van took me away from school, but the driver, Carrie, got stupid and didn't know the way home. I knew the way home. The place she was taking me wasn't it. I got scared and angry. I couldn't make sense of where we were going. I knew she was going the wrong way, but I couldn't get my mouth to tell her the words. Heck, I didn't even know I could use words to tell her what was wrong. I remembered my old driver who drove off the road to hit me. I melted down. I didn't have to go to the jail for PDD uneducable low-functioning autistic retards because I was in a car. I screamed and flailed around. I thought Carrie would hit me, but she didn't.

Instead, Carrie said I was dangerous, and I was going to cause an accident. The kids at school sometimes had accidents. An accident is what happens when someone poops and pees in their pants. I was four years old, and I was still in diapers. So how could I have an accident?

Matt and Danny rode in the van with me. They were scared and crying when all this happened. We finally arrived at a big house where Carrie dropped off Matt. Then she drove to my house. She told my mother I was dangerous and needed a "monitor" in the van. Carrie didn't like me, but she didn't hit me like the other van driver did. She told Danny and Matt's mothers I was a brat, and she wished I wasn't in her van. Carrie learned how to take me home the right way after that day, and never made the mistake again.

This wasn't the first time we had trouble in the van. Once Danny talked to me, and wanted me to talk back to him. He shouted into my ear, "TALK TO ME, YOU SILLY BOY." He hurt my ear by talking so loudly, and I couldn't talk anyway. I didn't know everything in the world had a name. I knew some words, but I couldn't make my mouth, tongue, and voice say the words. I knew people wanted something from me, but I didn't know what to do or how to do it. When he shouted in my ear, I hated it. I screamed, and I hit and scratched him. I tried to bite him too, but he was too far away. After that, he couldn't sit next to me. I missed him sitting next to me. I liked the way he said math facts the whole ride up. I couldn't hear him when he sat far from me.

After Carrie forgot the way home that time, Mommy had a fight with the school district. After the fight, a woman named Kathy rode on the van with us. I don't think she did much except sit there. Carrie did all of the driving. Kathy was a "monitor" and for years, she needed training, but she never got any.

Chapter 7: Toilet Torture

Abie's Thoughts

Speaking of training and accidents…. real people want retards to make sure their poop and pee goes into a toilet. Toileting has a special meaning to real people. I don't understand why. I'm used to making poop and pee go in the toilet. I like doing it that way because that's the way I normally do it.

I learned where to put poop and pee when I was four and a half years old. I didn't go by myself. Instead, I held it in until someone took me there. I was older when I learned I could go to the bathroom whenever I wanted. A few years later, I realized I was supposed to get out of bed to go to do this in the nighttime. Mommy and Daddy wanted me to stay in bed to go to sleep. It didn't make sense I could get out of bed to go to the bathroom. Real people say this is "an exception to the rule." I have problems understanding "an exception to the rule." It means there's a rule, but it can be broken. It's not really a rule if you can break it.

To get ready for toilet training, Mommy bought a huge pile of training pants, many cartons of delicious drinks such as chocolate milk, salty snacks, and a nice stimmer. The nice stimmer was a snake that shook like crazy when I waved it in front of my eyes. She also got a little toilet called a "potty." It was stupid because it didn't know how to flush.

To teach me to use a potty, a lady named Brendy came over to our house. She gave me orders because she was the boss. Mommy did the work, and Brendy gave the orders. Mommy didn't like the way she gave her orders. But Mommy said Brendy knew her stuff, and we just had to put up with it.

Mommy wanted her to make friends with me before she started bossing me around. She didn't.

She made me sit on the potty for a half hour and drink some nice drinks. Then I got off the potty and worked on imitation and other things for five minutes or so. Every minute, I got a cheese curl for having dry pants, and if I made anything in the toilet, I got the major reward, a stimmer for five minutes. If I peed or pooped on the floor, I got "a correction." That meant I had to go back to the potty for a lesson on sitting on it. As time went on, the time off the toilet got longer and longer, and the time between getting rewards for dry pants increased. More and more pee and poop ended up in the potty. The grown-up real people were happy about this. I didn't care, but I enjoyed getting the rewards.

A person and a fox thought up how to toilet train people like me. The name of the person was Nathan Azrin. If you don't know who he is, you can look him up on your computer. Just search for "Azrin and Foxx toilet training." He and a fox thought up the way to toilet train PDD uneducable low-functioning autistic retards. I'm not sure whether he was afraid of the fox, or whether the fox was the same one from the *Fox and the Hound*. I'm also not sure of how the fox helped him think up this way of toilet training. Perhaps the fox did the peeing and the pooping.

When Mommy got tired of taking me to the potty on a schedule, she taught me to walk to the potty further and further away from the bathroom instead of taking me there. When she did this, I got the idea I could go to the potty whenever I wanted to go from whatever location I happened to be. She called this "self-initiation." After a while, I used the regular toilet instead of a potty. My tushy got big when I was five, big enough to use a real toilet. The real toilet could flush, but I never flushed it. I noticed the grown-up real people wanted to look at my poop and pee. For some reason, they found it very interesting, so I left it for them to look at. Mommy put some expensive B6 and magnesium vitamins in my food. This turned my pee bright yellow. The vitamins were supposed to improve me, but never did. She always said I had the most expensive pee in all of Newtucktin. No wonder she wanted to look at it.

During the time we worked on toilet training with Brendy, Mommy spent about a month with me in the bathroom. She called it "toilet torture." We worked on toilet training from the time I woke up until the time I went to sleep whenever I didn't have school. I still had "accidents," but I learned what I was supposed to do.

Mommy and Brendy wrote down all sorts of numbers about my toilet training. I was still in diapers when I went to school. I couldn't figure out why. This was very confusing. Did they want me to pee and poop in the toilet or in a diaper? Real people have trouble making up their minds. I have no trouble making up my mind. I want what I want when I want it.

Arlene's Thoughts

After about a month of toilet training, I had data to show that Abie should be out of diapers in school. However, the data was mostly mine…from after school, before home program hours and on weekends. The data from the home program was not enough to satisfy Patricia Stone's requirements.

Brendy knew it was time for them to switch to training pants in the school, but her job was in the home program. "Yeah, it does seem that Abie's ready, but that's really the school's decision." She didn't want to get involved.

I called Patricia Stone.

"I can't switch him into training pants in school because I don't have the data to show he's ready," she said.

"I have the data."

"I need RELIABLE data."

"What do you consider reliable data?"

"Abie's data is good, but we need data that's been supervised by a qualified professional. When you're finished with the home program, we'll take him out of diapers in the school…regardless of the data. If you want to curtail your home programming a few months, we'll take him out of diapers."

I wanted to do a six-month home program. In order to get them to help with training in the school, I had to curtail the program to four months. This didn't make sense to me, but I agreed to shorten the home programming so Abie wouldn't get confused.

The toileting data issue was my first taste of what I called "the burden of proof." Everything a parent teaches his or her child with autism is in question and needs special proof for some professionals to accept it. Even with proof, the professionals may not accept a previously attained skill if taught by parents. If the professionals did not accept that the child had the skill, the child could spend many years working on a skill he already had. He'd never get an opportunity to move on.

Chapter 8: Progress and a Step Backward

Arlene's Thoughts

By the end of Abie's first year at the Behavioral School, he was somewhat toilet trained on a schedule. He could construct a block tower and train. He could do simple puzzles and the shape box within a discrete trial session. Unfortunately he didn't developed an interest in playing with blocks or puzzles outside of a teaching session.

He was able to do simple imitation and had picture recognition. His hand washing was less than perfect. The hand washing skill would reappear on his IEP more than a few dozen other times. He could follow a handful of one-step directions. He understood at least thirty words I taught him, but his receptive pointing seemed inaccurate. Speaking of pointing, I was able to get him to point to things he wanted by morphing the" give" sign into a point. He repeated the sounds for "K," "B" and "D." Thanks to Maureen, he was able to nod "yes" and shake his head "no." I also taught Abie to cut with a scissors during that year. This progress wouldn't place Abie into the category of miracle kid, but nevertheless, it was pretty good progress.

The Behavioral School had extinguished Abie's spit stim behaviors, but a new behavior took its place. The new behavior was equally disconcerting. This became a pattern....extinguish one behavior, and another takes its place. It was hardly worth it to work on extinguishing self-stimulatory behaviors because of this, but the school considered working on behaviors to be their foremost concern. The out-of-seat behavior had improved as well, but still needed work.

Unfortunately, with all these gains, he still had no play behavior, and he still didn't speak. He participated in a study regarding play behavior sponsored by the Behavioral School. His data counted as a successful outcome. He was able to imitate certain play actions on cue, but didn't explore his world by playing. The researcher counted this as attainment of play behavior. I didn't see how this counted as play behavior. Going through the motions of play behavior is not the same as real play.

I wondered what the next step was for language after learning those three sounds. Even though he reached the dreaded age of five, I was still hopeful he could progress significantly. The idea that Abie would someday have a normal life began to fade. Now the goal was just getting him to reach his own potential. But even that wasn't easy to do.

Patricia notified me that Abie would be moving out of the preschool program and into the school age program. I had no input into the decision to change Abie from one classroom to another. Abie never made it to the integrated classroom. After the fateful conversation with Mandy Greenberg, I knew he would never get there.

Patricia didn't show me the school age program when I first visited the school. I never would have switched schools if I had seen the classroom he was about to join. There were nine children in the classroom and three adults. It was chaotic, and quite loud. I asked the new teacher, Lynda, about getting together before the IEP team meeting. She told me everything was already all set.   That was definitely a red flag for me. I didn't want them meeting and deciding everything beforehand without my input.

The day of the team meeting, Jon and I walked into a room with ten professionals. These were Patricia Stone, the director, and Lynda, the head teacher and case worker, a speech therapist, an occupational therapist, a social worker, a physical therapist, the program coordinator, the assistant director of the school program, an intern, and Mary Carpenter, the liaison from the school district. Similar to our first meeting with the school district, I didn't know many people at the meeting. These professionals seemed unfamiliar with Abie. He never received a physical therapy or a physical therapy consult or evaluation, so it seemed very strange to have a physical therapist at the meeting. That year the occupational therapist and speech therapist didn't work with Abie. Instead, they provided a consultation to the classroom. I couldn't imagine the participants in the meeting engaging Abie in anything. This was common for all his subsequent IEP meetings. There were many "expert" opinions from folks who probably never came within twenty feet of a child with severe autism. I never thought such people should have a say, but those were the folks who had the power. I called them "meeting goers" because you would only see them at meetings. You would never actually catch them working with a child.

From the outset, the meeting didn't look promising. Instead of Mary Carpenter leading the meeting, Patricia Stone was the facilitator.

Patricia began her speech. "We've done an outstanding job with Abie this past year. He's progressed with most of his goals. As you might know, the federal department of education has cited our state for not including parents within the IEP process. Of course, unlike the rest of the state, here at the Behavioral School, parents have always been an integral part of our program. Our family advisory committee chaired by a wonderful parent and advocate, Darlene Diamond…that's Matt's mom… provides parent and family insight and advice into all our programming. We work side-by-side with the parents in our home program. Our satisfaction survey shows that parents love our services. At the Behavioral School, they can be certain we do everything possible for their loved one.

Because the feds have noticed other programs around the state have failed to do what we have done for many years, they have introduced a new IEP form. This form will facilitate the inclusion of parents in the IEP process. Instead of having a simple IEP with goals and short-term objectives, the new IEP form includes the parents' vision for the child, areas of concern, and present levels of performance. These items drive the IEP process. I invite everyone to look Abie's IEP over now. Patricia handed Jon and me a copy of a filled-in IEP. The papers were marked "proposed draft."

Then I spoke. "Don't we get any input into the process?"

Patricia replied. "Yes, of course. That's what this meeting is all about. We certainly didn't want to waste everyone's time by coming to this meeting and not having at least some idea of what should be on the plan. Therefore, we took the initiative and filled out the IEP form beforehand. However, this is just a draft. Obviously the parents play a key role and may still provide input."

I looked down where it said "Parent/Student Vision," and then I asked, "Shouldn't the vision actually be the vision the family has for their child?"

"Our families are not professionals. They don't have the formal training to describe a realistic vision for a disabled child. They need help from us. The concerns section is similar. We know what the families' concerns should be. We've worked closely with your child, and we can accurately predict your child's trajectory with exceptional precision."

I glanced at the IEP. "The IEP has a goal ….Abraham will hold a scissors correctly. The present levels of performance say Abie cannot cut or hold a scissors correctly. Abie can already cut with a scissors."

"You are the parents, so you know your child best. However, we've tested Abie. He can't hold a scissors, let alone make a cut. All the professionals here can attest to the fact that Abie cannot cut with a scissors," Patricia replied. Everyone except Jon and I vigorously nodded their heads in agreement.

Then I looked over at the television and the VCR in the corner of the room. "Does the television and VCR work?"

Patricia's face looked confused. "Yes, of course. We do trainings using the TV and VCR. Sometimes we record the students and troubleshoot issues."Her face changed to anger as soon as she saw what I was about to do.

"Excellent. I'll show you Abie cutting with a scissors," I said.

I had a huge bag with me. It contained a concealed video tape. From my experience with the home program, I had an inkling I was going to have to prove Abie had some of the skills he had. All eyes were on me as I removed the videotape from my purse. Clearly, they weren't expecting this. I popped the tape into the VCR player and turned the television on. All the meeting participants except for Jon sat there with their mouths open. The first clip showed Abie with a scissors cutting some paper. He wasn't struggling. He clearly knew what he was doing. I felt triumphant. I proved Abie could cut with a scissors. My opinion counted.

Then I noticed Patricia and her crew all shooting me a look that could kill. Jon looked back at them, and his face turned white. He looked as if he might pass out. In a split second, I realized I made a terrible mistake.

Then Lynda said in a condescending tone, "Mrs. Dancer, we would be happy to strike the holding the scissors goal from Abie's IEP if that's what you want, but you should know he hasn't generalized this skill to our environment. Generalization is a very concerning problem children diagnosed with autism tend to have. I strongly recommend you keep this goal in the IEP as it stands."

Then Patricia piped in and stared at me. "I seem to remember last year YOU wanted to put an imitation goal into the IEP because Abie hadn't generalized a skill to the home environment. I believe we have the same issue here with the scissors skills."

"Is it possible to replace this goal? How about changing the levels of performance section?" I replied.

"We'll be happy to add the sentence: 'The parents report emerging scissors skills.' However, we wouldn't want to replace the scissors goal. We'd just work harder at the remaining goals. In a way, it's an advantage for Abie to have fewer goals on the IEP. That way we can work harder on the ones we have, and thus have a better chance of progress and success. It's your choice, Mrs. Dancer. You're an important member of this team."

"Is it possible to get rid of this goal and replace it with something else?" I asked.

Patricia frowned, and answered angrily. "I've already answered that question. We can strike the goal from the IEP or keep it in. We will not replace the goal because in my professional opinion, it's wrong and unethical to do so."

I had a hard time digesting the argument. After all, this was about cutting with a scissors, not about confirming Abie as justice of the Supreme Court. I thought it best to move on. "Okay. Let's move on. There are no speech goals here."

"Yes, there's a communication goal here created by our speech therapist, Cindy. Cindy, do you want to explain?" Lynda replied.

"Yes, since Abie hasn't developed oral speech, we've decided to concentrate on using the communication board. Studies have proven that using a communication board does nothing to prevent a person from developing oral speech. In fact, using an alternative mode of communication could actually facilitate speech. We'll be giving Abie an alternative means of communication in case his speech does not come in. At five years old it's extremely unlikely Abie will ever develop oral speech."

It seemed to me there was a self-fulfilling prophesy here. If the professionals gave up on oral speech at the age of five, it made sense that it was unlikely it would happen. Besides, Cindy never worked with Abie...not even once.

"What do you normally do when a young child learns to imitate sounds and he or she is less than age five? What are the next steps?" I asked.

"There are no next steps other than using a communication board. Either a person develops speech or he or she doesn't. Your child didn't develop speech, is nonverbal, and will never develop speech in my professional opinion. We are very honest in our program. We don't give parents false hope like some other programs out there."

"But what would you do if he weren't five years old?"

"He IS five years old. Five years old is the cut off."

"When a student who is under five years old imitates many sounds, then what do you do?"

"Nothing. Either the kid speaks or he doesn't."

It sounded to me like they did not have a comprehensive system of working on the development of speech and language.

Throughout the meeting, Mary Carpenter remained silent. In addition to placing students, her job was to oversee the private placements and make sure that they were actually doing what the school district was paying them to do. I turned my head and looked at Mary Carpenter.

She looked around at the meeting participants. "I've been very impressed with the professionalism at the Behavioral School. I believe the proposed IEP is excellent, and I thank you all for your hard work. I'm going to need to go to my next appointment soon, so I hope we can hurry this along a bit. In any case I'll need to slip out in about two minutes." She never actually glanced at the IEP or looked at anything except the face page. She left the meeting exactly two minutes after she made that statement.

Jon finally chimed in. "The present levels of performance aren't accurate in many other cases in the IEP."

"I assure you, Mr. Dancer, they are quite accurate," Patricia replied.

Then the social worker threw her nose in the air and looked down on Jon and me. "Mr. and Mrs. Dancer, you have an opportunity to look over the IEP as we have written it. If you have any problem with the IEP as it has been written, you are asking for a new placement."

I was shocked and unprepared for those words. "A new placement?"

"Yes, we've decided what Abie's levels of performance are and what his needs are. We are ready to deliver it. Anything less than what we have outlined in this IEP plan would be unethical. Therefore, we wouldn't be able to carry it out. So either you sign this as is, or we can no longer serve your son."

"So what input do we as parents actually have?"

"You have the opportunity to accept or reject the plan, but please know if you reject the plan or you partially reject the plan, you are asking for a new placement," Patricia replied.

This was very different from what Patricia Stone told me when we were considering the Behavioral School. It was also different from when we first entered the school. I realized at that point why so many families left. I felt sad Abie hadn't bonded with any of the staff at the school the way he had bonded with Elsa, Candy, and Maureen.

But still, the Behavioral School had a way of getting Abie to cooperate by being willing to add the motivation Abie was lacking. He did learn some skills during that first year at there. Cognitive Kids seemed to be running out of ideas by the time we left.

In subsequent years, the school allowed us to write the vision statement and the parental concerns in the IEP, but they never used any of that information. Otherwise, the IEP process went similarly to this meeting. Every year the school decided whatever they wanted to put on the IEP. There was always a threat of termination ready in case there was any disagreement. Many times, they told us how wonderful they were. They said how they accomplished this or that goal. Then a few years later, we'd see that very same goal back on the IEP. There was no accountability in the system. However, a few angels showed up from time to time. These angels kept my hope going. There were also a few more opportunities yet to come.

Enrolling Abie in an autism school program was more like joining a cult. Questioning, criticizing, or contradicting the school gurus was a terrible sin, which could be punished by excommunication. The school expected parents to accept their opinions and dictates blindly and with faith, and without questioning.

Chapter 9: The New Classroom

Abie's Thoughts

Jenny and the two aides in my old classroom never said goodbye to me when I moved to the new classroom. I still saw them in the hallway, but they never talked to me ever again. Only Maureen Pauley said "hi" when she saw me. All three of my old teachers were going to have babies. When their bellies got big, they left the school completely and never came back. My new teacher, Lynda, was also pregnant. She lost one baby, so she was extra careful not to work too hard. I wondered where she lost the baby. I think if a person lost a baby, the baby should be easy to find because it would cry. Babies make annoying sounds, just like retards do. Everyone likes babies, but they sure don't like PDD uneducable low functioning autistic retards.

The new classroom was very noisy all the time. There were nine retards in there and three teachers. I want to tell you what November 15th in 1993 was like. That was a Monday, but every day in that classroom was like that Monday.

We all got to school and went into the classroom. Michael took out his communication book from his pocket. He pointed to water in his communication book. Then he raised his hand and then pointed again to water in his book. The teachers didn't see him do this because they were talking to each other.

I couldn't get him water because I was a PDD uneducable low-functioning autistic retard, so don't blame me. He got mad because he was thirsty, and couldn't get any water. He pounded the table. Mark was sitting next to him, so he punched Mark because he didn't get him water. Mark was also a retard and five years old like me, and couldn't get him water. A retard like Mark wouldn't think about getting someone else water anyway. Mark started crying because Michael hit him, but Michael kept on hitting him.

Then Jeff and Greg made loud vocal self-stim noises. I suppose the noises blocked out Mark's crying, but it sounded like screaming and made the situation worse. Finally, this caught the teachers' attention. They looked at Michael, but they didn't get him water. The three of them ran over to Michael, grabbed him, and forced him to lie down on his stomach on the floor. It looked like they were sitting on top of him. Then two teachers dragged him away. Michael was crying very loudly, and flailing about. I know where the teachers took him... the jail for PDD uneducable low-functioning autistic retards, and they probably shut the door for a long time. While all of this was happening, Ashley pulled her pants down for no particular reason and flapped her hand in front of her face. Then Eddie started to smell bad because he probably pooped in his pants. Joey looked at the windows and the doors. He probably had a plan to escape any minute. The smell from Eddie was so bad, so who could blame Joey. Sam just sat there saying, "Captain, there's trouble on deck. Red Alert."

In that classroom, there were always "behaviors." One kid would have a tantrum, and that caused others to act up. Eventually we all were acting up or we were melting down like the wicked witch. I couldn't stand it. Once I arrived at school, my only thought was how in the world I can block this whole thing out of my mind. I looked for stimmers, grabbed stimmers, stimmed on someone's hair, and waved my hands in front of my eyes for hours in order to block this all out.

The teachers, Lynda and Carla, spent a lot of time talking to each other. The other teacher, Laverne Yakazuki, tried very hard to teach us some things. She tried to get me to put on my shoes and tie them. I did learn to put on my shoes, but sometimes I put the wrong shoe on the wrong foot. I couldn't concentrate enough to actually tie the shoes. It was just too noisy.

Sometimes Lynda tried to get me to use the communication board. Once, when I felt like throwing up, Lynda tried to get me to use the communication board. She made me point to cheese curl over and over again, and then made me eat the cheese curls. I didn't want them even though I liked cheese curls. I just wanted to go home. I had a tantrum, and ended up in the jail for PDD uneducable low-functioning autistic retards. She left me there alone for a long time. I tried to get out, but she locked the door. I threw up there, and then I stimmed on the throw up. I had diarrhea, but I couldn't go to a bathroom because I was in the jail. So I went in my pants, and it rolled down my legs. I tried to get it off my legs, but it ended up all over the place. Lynda finally opened the door to let me out. When she saw me, she shouted, "Laverne! Laverne! Come here with some gloves on."

Mommy picked me up an hour after that. When she saw me with poop and throw up in my hair, lots of tears dripped down her eyes. She put down a towel in the car for the long drive home. I had a bath at home, and Mommy washed my hair. She hugged me and told me that she loved me. I wasn't sure what that meant. I pushed her away from me because I felt something strong about her. It almost made me cry, but I didn't understand it. I backed away for a second. Then I hugged her with all my might and I didn't want to let go for a long time. From then on, I thought that Mommy's job was to help and protect me. After that, whenever I wanted something, I looked her straight in the eye. Too bad there wasn't a way to tell her exactly how I wanted her to help me, but most of the time, I knew she would if she could.

When I came home from school, Mommy said I looked like a stimmed out zombie. She gave me a drink, and then took me right upstairs for discrete trials in my room. I was used to blocking out the world by stimming all day in school. It was harder than ever to pay attention. We worked on the same things over and over again. It was like I was there, yet I wasn't. I hardly ever got anything right. One day she sat in the little chair opposite me and she cried. The tears rolled down her face while I flapped my hands in front of my face. Then Daddy came home.

That weekend Daddy brought me into my room, and sat me at the little table. He had a stack of plates with him. They were bright and colorful. Red, yellow, and blue. Wow, this was new.... having Daddy work with me instead of Mommy. I don't like new things, but I sure did like Daddy working with me. He liked children, but I think he liked real children, not retards like me.... but maybe he did like me after all. He worked with me for hours until I sorted the plates perfectly. He told Mommy I had intelligence in my eyes, and I could learn if only I had the right kind of help. If only, we knew the right way to reach me. Working with Daddy and the plates was the happiest time I had that year and perhaps in my whole life

At the end of that year, many white hands attached to white ladies tested me, and saw how good I was at sorting. They liked to teach me sorting all the time because I already knew how to do that. The teachers liked to say they taught me sorting, but Daddy really taught me sorting.

After I went to the new classroom, Mommy was very tired and sad so she looked for other people to work with me instead of her. She took me to speech therapy and occupational therapy in a big office building. At speech therapy, I saw many people Mommy and I knew.

One time, Mommy was sick with a fever, so Maureen Pauley took me to speech therapy instead. I liked going with Maureen. She asked me if I wanted to use a vending machine before my speech therapy session began. I didn't know what a vending machine was, but Maureen always knew how to have fun. So I nodded "yes" just the way she taught me. When she saw me nod "yes," she smiled and gave me a high five. I smiled too. The vending machines were really something. They had sodas, pretzels, chips, candy.... basically anything a real kid or a retard kid could ever want. The goodies were behind glass so you couldn't just take one. People were putting money into a slot. Then they pushed a button next to the treat they wanted. Then it came out of a slot on the bottom.

Matt was there with his mother, Darlene, and they were getting a treat for him.

Maureen pointed to crackers inside the vending machine. "Peanut butter" was clearly written on the wrapper." So Abie, do you want these crackers?" She watched carefully as she pointed to see if I would follow her point with my eyes. Oh yes, I wanted the crackers with the peanut butter in them.

I nodded.

"Yes, what? Yes, Abie wants........."

"Cra ca," I answered by filling in the blank. Maureen's face looked like a happy face when I said that.

"Abie, good job. You deserve a cracker, now. Here's your

money." Maureen handed me four quarters, but I didn't know what to do. She pointed to the slot. I tried to put the money in. I had a little trouble, but she helped me get the money in the slot. Then she waited to see if I would press the right button. I tried to, but I didn't press it hard enough. She put her hand behind mine and helped me press. Then the crackers came out of the slot.

"Hey cutie. How about that?" She tickled me and gave me a high five as she handed me the crackers.

Matt's mother was watching us the whole time. She walked over to us and spoke to Maureen. "Hi, I want to introduce myself. I'm Darlene Diamond, the head of the Behavioral School's parent advisory committee. I'm Matt's mother. I must say you do a wonderful job with your little friend."

"Thank you. I believe we've met before. I'm Maureen, Abie's babysitter. I'm also a teacher in the integrated classroom at the Behavioral School. Matt was just transitioning out of the integrated preschool classroom into the school-age program when I came to work there. I remember him." She bent down to Matt's height . "Hi there, Matt."

Matt looked at his mother instead of Maureen. "Hi!" he said.

"Matt's made some great progress lately. Have you noticed? Having someone like you as a respite worker or a tutor could really be good for him. It would be great if you could work for us," Darlene said.

"I've have noticed Matt's improvement, and I think that's wonderful. I'd love to work with Matt, but I'm already working full time for the Behavioral School. I've been doing respite for the Dancers about once a month and for another family once a week on a regular basis. I couldn't take another respite job right now, but thanks so much."

"Wait a minute. You should reconsider. You could drop one of your current respite jobs to work for us. Matt, is higher functioning and has fewer behaviors than your little friend has. He's much easier to work with. I'm getting more funding than the Dancers are, and I can supplement your pay with some of my own money. I'm sure you have student loans to pay off. Our house is large, and it has a pool. The working conditions are so much better than what you're probably getting at the Dancers or with the other family. Also, I could also put in a good word for you at the Behavioral School. Did I mention I chair the parent advisory committee? Why don't you just give me your number?"

"Sorry. I'm already committed."

"Okay, here's my number. Call me if you change your mind. The Dancers or your other family can find another respite worker. You shouldn't worry too much about them. You should just do what's best for you. I'm heading back to Matt's session. Think about it." Then she walked off while she dragged Matt by the hand.

After they were gone, Maureen talked to me as if I was a grown up real person. "What a piece of work, trying to steal a respite worker from another family. I guess she's just desperate. I wouldn't work for her even if she paid me a million bucks. Let's go, Abie."

The speech therapy session was always the same. The therapist brought out a cardboard with symbols and words underneath the symbols. Each symbol represented an activity. I pointed to an activity and then the activity happened. The symbols never actually looked like the item or the activity, but after a while I was able to read the words under the symbol. Nobody including my parents knew I was reading those words. Mommy said she didn't know what I really got out of speech therapy. Whatever it was, it was better than stimming myself silly.

Mommy and Daddy also brought me to an occupational therapist. This was my most fun activity. Not only was it fun for me, but my parents always said they had fun too. My occupational therapist, Julie, taught me buttoning. She also taught me how to do many things with my hands. After I worked with my hands, I got to swing on the wide variety of swings. Sometimes she put lotion on my hands and feet. Mommy and Daddy spoke to Julie's husband during my therapy. We always left happy. When I started doing a good job with zipping and buttoning, I ended up having an occupational therapist at school too. They called her OT. OT took a special interest in me because she saw how fast I learned things. I was fast on learning these things because I was working with Julie too. After all, for all of the other things, I was a slow low-functioning uneducable autistic retard. After a while, my parents stopped taking me to occupational therapy. Mommy said something about the insurance not paying enough for this. Then I didn't see Julie again just like I didn't see Elsa, Candy and Dr. Smith.

Chapter 10: Nowhere to Go

Arlene's Thoughts

The years passed, and I worked with Abie as hard as I could. At times, I lost steam, and then somehow I would regain my motivation. I lost hope that the school would provide what he needed. However, from time to time, there was a teacher or a therapist who took an interest in him. When this happened, my hope would bloom a little, only to die off once that teacher or therapist left the school. I thought Abie could progress so much more if he had the right intervention. I no longer hoped he would become normal or he would reach his own potential. Those were pipe dreams. I just wanted him to be in an environment where he could progress at least a tiny bit. I wanted him in a place where they cared for him and treated him like a human being. He was a heavy-duty kid. I couldn't do it myself. I needed help.

We looked into other programming, but most of the other schools told us their wait lists were so long it didn't pay to consider them. However, the New Progress School was interested in talking to us. I was elated when they told us they wanted us to come in and talk to them about a possible placement for Abie.

Both Jon and I wondered whether the New Progress School would be any different from the Behavioral School. Their philosophies and reputations seemed similar.

At the New Progress School, a woman named Marcy met us at the reception area. She escorted us to observe a classroom through a one-way glass. She didn't offer us chairs. We observed two students working in discrete trial sessions. The students appeared to be paying attention and learning. Each student was working with a teacher one-to-one. Marcy looked at her watch every few minutes. When we observed for exactly fifteen minutes, she brought us into a conference room where we met another woman named Barbara.

Marcy spoke first. "We are the premier clinical setting for the treatment of children diagnosed with autism and related disorders. There is no better school option for someone diagnosed with autism in the United States and probably, the world. We are an applied behavior analysis or ABA school, and we base all of our work on behavioral science. Our students work in small groups of three with a three to one ratio."

I interjected. "Excuse me. I have a question. If we can get the school system to pay for a one-to-one aide, can you accommodate that? We just observed a session where the students had one-to-one support."

"The missing students from that classroom were in the cafeteria. Those students don't normally have one-to-one instruction. We would not be able to accommodate a one-to-one. Just think about it. If a student got funded for a one-to-one aide, two other students would get a one-to-two ratio without their school districts paying for the additional service."

"Wouldn't that be better for them? Wouldn't they make more progress?" I asked.

"That's not the point. The school district would be getting a service they're not paying for. They would be getting something for nothing. Whether or not that would be beneficial to the students is irrelevant."

Red flags were waving. This organization had agendas aside from helping the students. I wanted to get Abie out of the Behavioral School, so I tried to ignore the glaring red flags, but they kept on waving.

"We might consider putting your son on our wait list, but we would need a commitment. You must agree to send him here when his name comes up on our wait list," Marcy said.

"Well, since you don't have an actual opening, and can't promise us an opening at a particular time, we want to look into other programs." Marcy shot us a nasty look, and I realized I shouldn't have said that.

"We're only interested in families who are committed to our program. We're not interested in families who are considering other programs," she said.

"Well, can you offer us placement now?"

Barbara answered. "No. We might be able to offer the wait list if your son is suitable for our program. We have a very long wait list, and we place only the most promising candidates on our list."

"If we went on the wait list, how long a wait would it be?"

"It could be anywhere between one year and five years. In some cases we might decide not to take him when his name came up,"

"If you have the right to decide not to take him, why can't we look into other alternatives? It hardly seems fair."

"This is what you must do if you want a chance to get into our award-winning, world famous program. Families who send their children here have an opportunity to get the best," said Barbara.

"In our program we provide an annual comprehensive assessment for your son. His IEP would be based on a combination of our curriculum and where we think he is, based on our assessment," said Marcy.

"What if another evaluator recommends something not in your curriculum?" asked Jon.

"Oh, we wouldn't have to worry about that. Our evaluators would never suggest something not in our curriculum."

"I was talking about an outside evaluator. For instance, Abie sees a neurologist, Dr. Doris Treisman. What if she recommended something?"

"If your son attended our school, he wouldn't need to see any professionals outside our school."

"We would still take him to see his neurologist. We need the opinion of an outside person."

"We're really only interested in having families who are committed to our philosophy and our professionals. We're the best of the best, and only the best are associated with us. You don't need anyone else. Besides, all our professionals work together. We have physicians we use. If we decided to take your son, he would use our physicians," Marcy explained.

"Is your son verbal? What kind of social skills does he have, and what grade level is he academically?" Barbara asked.

"Abie speaks softly in a whisper in an inarticulate way. Not many people understand him, and some professionals don't recognize his verbal speech as speech. Besides, he doesn't talk much anyway. He never developed play behavior. He is not in a particular grade level, and he doesn't socialize with his peers," I answered.

"Mr. and Mrs. Dancer, we don't seem to have a match here. Abie is too low functioning to be in our program, and you don't seem all that committed to our approach. I don't think this is going to work."

I was disappointed even though I knew Barbara was right. The school was not a match for us. The situation was too similar to the program we had him in already. There was no reason to uproot him to attend the New Progress School. I knew many lower functioning children who were attending the New Progress School. However, Barbara and Marcy may have overlooked some of our "lack of commitment" had Abie been higher functioning.

It was a shame to have Abie travel around an hour back and forth to his program. The Behavioral School wasn't helping him. The school district together with help from the state paid over six figures for tuition and transportation for him. Those figures seemed outrageous.

I thought, "How can those figures be right when there are aides in the school making $10 per hour?" We couldn't get Abie into another private school. It was time to return Abie back to the school district. I called the principal of the local middle school, Emily Fairfield, and asked for an appointment.

Jon was skeptical about the local school handling Abie, but education in the least restrictive environment was Abie's right. The public school was considered a less restrictive environment than a private specialty school. Perhaps they'd learn to handle him.

I thought some of Abie's behaviors were due to his attending the Behavioral School. He was unhappy there, and his unhappiness showed up in his behaviors.

My first appointment with the Emily went well. She told me all about children with autism they included in the school. She seemed excited at the prospect of bringing Abie to the public school. She told me she needed to contact the Behavioral School to get more information. She'd get back to me. I was happy and hopeful at the prospect of Abie attending his neighborhood school. I had many ideas about how to integrate him into our community. I was excited, and for the first time in a long time, I had hope.

After Emily's discussion with Patricia Stone of the Behavioral School, her enthusiasm for including Abie in the public school turned sour. She called and said she wouldn't be able to handle him in the public school because of his behaviors. Patricia described Abie as dangerous, and needing regular physical restraints. I told Emily, "Abie lives at home with us, two five-foot weaklings, and we handle him just fine." Finally she said, "I don't want him in this school, and the school system is willing to pay anything to keep him out."

"I don't think you should lend too much credence to Ms. Stone's report. After all, the Behavioral School gets a lot of money to keep Abie. They don't want the money to walk out the door," I said.

"The Behavioral School has a great reputation and a wait list a mile long. They don't need your business. However, even if that's true, I don't want to take the risk. I don't want your son here. You're better off keeping him where they want him, rather than trying to send him to a school where they don't. Think about it. I'm sorry things didn't work out, but I hope you won't waste your money and the school system's money trying to fight my decision."

"I don't know what to say or what my next move will be, but I'm very sad about how this worked out."

"I am too. Goodbye." Then she hung up and the discussion regarding Abie attending the local public school was over.

Emily Fairfield was willing to make this judgment about Abie based solely on Patricia Stone's words. Emily never met Abie, but she denied him the right to attend the school in his district. Jon said it was all for the best. Emily would have kicked Abie out of the school at the first sign of trouble anyway.

The next day in the local paper there was a huge article about the local middle school principal, Emily Fairfield. The article said she was a champion for students with disabilities. She turned no one away. "The Newtucktin School District is a model for full inclusion," the article stated. "All students regardless of disability are welcomed here. There are no exceptions."

Some of my neighbors knew I was looking for a new placement for Abie. One of them pointed out the article to me. She didn't believe me when I told her that Emily Fairfield, the champion for children with disabilities, told me the school district would pay anything to keep Abie out of the public schools.

I decided not to fight Emily Fairfield's decision. We would have needed a separate room where an aide could work with Abie, and many other accommodations too. We would have needed the school's commitment to educating him. Otherwise, the situation just wouldn't work.

I asked Mary Carpenter if there were any other options for Abie. She knew of a private school for autism with openings. This school used painful aversive therapy with electric shock treatments that left burn marks on arms and legs. I wasn't interested.

I also asked Mary Carpenter about the possibility of having a one-to-one home program for Abie instead of a school-based program. In those days, insurance didn't pay for ABA home treatment. There were very few autism home providers for school age children, although that was soon to change. The home program run by the Behavioral School was restricted to preschoolers. The public school would have had to run a home program for Abie directly rather than contracting the service out to a corporate provider.

Mary Carpenter said the school department could not run a home program directly because of possible lawsuits. The school believed that a one-to-one aide working in my home would not be safe. Of course, the aide would not have been alone. I would have been there.

I had only two choices, keep Abie at the Behavioral School or take him out and work with him myself at home. If I took him out, I would have had absolutely no support except for five hours of respite per month. It would have been impossible.

Our decision was to keep Abie at the Behavioral School and to look for ways to increase his skill level by working with him outside of school.

Abie's Thoughts

Mowgli must leave the jungle and go to the man village. The jungle is not the place for him. He can't stay with Baloo, the bear. He has to go to the man village and be with other man-childs. By man-childs, they mean real man-childs, not retards. Retards belong in a special retard man-village, not in a school for real children and not in the jungle. Real children and their parents don't want to see retards in the school, especially retards with PDD low functioning autistic behaviors.

I hated the retard school, and I bashed in walls every time I thought about going there. I hated myself because I was a PDD low functioning autistic retard. I bit my wrist and hit myself in the head. I knew that Mommy was mad at my school. That made me mad too.

Just because a kid goes to school doesn't mean he learns something there. And just because a kid doesn't learn anything at school doesn't mean he doesn't learn at all. This is true even if a kid is a PDD uneducable low functioning autistic retard.

Mommy said I had another plateau that lasted for years, but I didn't. She also said I was wasting my time watching the same videos over and over again. I didn't have the words to tell her, but as I watched those videos through the years, I learned more and more things. I watched Kidsongs and I learned the written words to sounds I heard by looking at the subtitles over and over again. I learned many other things too from watching movies and TV. I listened to real people even though it looked like I was tuning out and not paying attention. I learned. There was no plateau.

Chapter 11: The Secret

Abie's Thoughts

One day when Mommy was working with me, she asked me to point to a card that had a "ba" sound, so I pointed to "b." Then she wanted me to point to a "wa" sound, so I pointed to "w." Then she went on and on about other sounds in the alphabet. I got them all right, and Mommy gave me popcorn and raisins for doing this correctly.

Then she wrote some words on an index card, and asked me what it said.

My voice came out as a whisper. "Ca ya haads."

"Do it," said Mommy.

I looked around. Then I looked straight up at the ceiling. *Do it? Do what?*

"Do what it says on this card," said Mommy.

So, I clapped my hands. Then she asked me to read many cards, and she had me following directions from the cards. She seemed to be very excited and happy as we did this work. She wasn't expecting me to get the right answers. I thought that was funny so I laughed and laughed.

Then she tried to get me to type words into a computer. I couldn't do it, even though she begged me to do this. She bribed me with chocolates, but I still couldn't do it. There were just too many letters to choose from. It gave me a headache and made me confused.

She sat down with me and tried to get me to read, *Go Dog, Go.* I could read it, but I didn't want to. I didn't understand why she wanted me to read this book. Also, it was hard for me to make my mouth say the words.

The next day we worked on these same things and the day after that too. From then on, when I said something she couldn't understand, she wrote down two possibilities of what she thought I said. I would point to the right one.

Some people have hidden pasts and skeletons, which are dead people, in their closets. These have to be secrets. If someone tells these secrets, everyone will get into trouble. So they never tell anyone their secrets. My secret was I knew how to read. PDD low functioning autistic retards are not allowed to read, so we had to keep this a secret from everyone except for Daddy. If a PDD low functioning autistic retard is actually reading, that means the parents are delusional because no PDD low functioning autistic retard can read. That's why it's a secret. I don't know what "delusional" means, but it's something that a lot of parents of retards have.

Arlene's Thoughts

Anna had a website called *That Bitch Next Door.* Her next-door neighbor hated her autistic son, Max. She called him names, and complained every time Max played outside. She said Max made abnormal noises. She shouldn't be forced to listen to him. She called him names like "retard" every time he stepped outside. Anna posted all the nasty things her neighbor did to her family on that website. She recorded her neighbor's cruel voice, and put the audio on the website too. She had fun with it and told jokes about it. She made something upsetting into something hilarious.

Anna was my hero. She lived thousands of miles away, yet her experiences were similar to mine. I met Anna online, and communicated with her every day, sometimes on our online support group, and sometimes on personal email. I always knew I could count on her to help me when I was feeling down.

Anna had her fill of arrogant school administrators and school programming that didn't work. She simply pulled Max out of school, and taught him at home. In her state, she was able to get intensive wraparound services to help her at home for several hours a week. It was possible, but not easy, to do what she did. Unfortunately, in her dedication to her son and to others, she forgot one very important person, herself. She skipped colonoscopies prescribed by her doctor because she needed to teach Max. How I wish we could go back in time. I would have tried to convince her to take care of herself.

Anna suggested I teach Abie how to read. She said it would be a good tool for him. If I thought Abie wanted something, I could jot the words down on the fly and have him pick. "Maybe he'll learn to type independently," she said.

Anna not only gave me hope when I needed it most, but she gave me detailed lessons for teaching a low functioning non-verbal child how to read, starting with matching sounds to letters. Anna originally designed the reading program for her low functioning non-verbal son, Max. In defiance of the school system, she taught Max how to read. When he was in school, the administrators laughed at her when she suggested they teach Max how to read.

I knew Abie would never get an opportunity to learn to read at school either, so I took Anna's advice and her reading program. I expected to spend months teaching Abie her lessons. I thought it was going to be a very long tedious process, just like fill and pour or toilet training. I figured this was something I could try even though I would probably get frustrated and give up on it. But much to my surprise, we went through Anna's lessons like lightning. We did her whole plan, which should have taken months, in about a week. I couldn't understand it. Everything I taught Abie was an impossible chore, but this was a breeze. It seemed like he already knew how to read, and I was just finding out what he already knew.

When I realized what Abie's reading skills were, I pictured him telling me all sorts of things by typing into a computer. At last, he would be telling me everything. I saw other non-verbal autistic children and adults typing into a computer for communication. Unfortunately, Abie's skills only went so far. He couldn't type words independently and accurately even though he could read.

I did use his reading skills to clarify what he tried to say sometimes. Sometimes I wrote out instructions for him in order to help him learn a task. I debated whether to tell the school Abie knew how to read. His reading could help him learn other skills. However, I knew this would cause a huge commotion culminating in a scene similar to the one we had years ago with the scissors goal. I decided to keep Abie's reading skills quiet. Eventually someone would figure out he knew how to read. Then they could take credit for teaching him. It would be better for everyone concerned if they found out about this on their own.

I was very excited about Abie knowing how to read, even though this skill proved to be more of a parlor trick than a functional skill. Still, I was very grateful to Anna for helping me give Abie the chance to show me he knew this. Previously I thought he could not acquire knowledge unless someone taught it to him directly. Now I knew he was picking up information on his own.

I would have given anything to know what he actually knew. I would have given anything to know what he thought and how he experienced the world.

His IQ had been tested many times. He never cooperated with that kind of a test. So the professionals always said that his IQ was so low that he couldn't be tested. I wondered what his intelligence level really was. Perhaps that's what the real secret was.

Anna was dealt a very difficult lot in life, but she helped me and many other people too. She taught her son to read and to do many other things. Anna died at age 60 from terminal colon cancer that had metastasized. Sixty years old used to seem old. To me that age was too young to die, especially for someone as full of life as Anna. However, she did better with her sixty years in life than many people do with more years. She filled her life with meaning. She found humor in the face of despair. She was strong. She helped her family, and she helped others. It's not about your lot in life, but what you do with what you have.

Chapter 12: Advocacy Infusion

Arlene's Thoughts

Once a year we visited Abie's neurologist, Dr. Doris Treisman. She monitored Abie's progress and did whatever she could to help us.

At one of Abie's visits, she asked, "So how is everything going with Abie? What are they working on at school now?"

"Abie is eleven years old now, so the school insists on having vocational and transitional skills on his IEP."

"I think that community based instruction is very good for Abie. Working on potential job skills is beneficial as well."

"They don't do community based instruction, and the vocational skills amount to Abie taking a piece of paper and sticking it into a shredder. He doesn't stay with it for more than a few seconds, and they don't seem to have a strategy for expanding this time. It's useless, Dr. Treisman. I don't see much teaching or learning at the school. Abie comes home looking like he's been on drugs. I think it's from the lack of structure and all the stimming. He's become very hard to teach after school and on weekends. Also, we've had some problems with getting Abie to cooperate with the dentist."

She looked deep in thought and paused. "What kind of help do you have at home?"

"Basically none. We do get some respite…..about 5 hours a month. I try to work with Abie around two hours after school and about five hours or so each day on the weekends. After about two hours of discrete trials, I get very tired, but I continue pushing him in the natural environment. Whatever Abie learns, he learns from me. The school is important because I need a break. It's respite for me."

"You shouldn't even be trying to do this whole thing yourself. You need help…much more help than you're getting. Tell me about the issues with the dentist. I don't think I remember the details. Have you tried the Special Needs Dental Clinic?"

"We started out with a pediatric dentist when Abie was very young, but he couldn't handle Abie. Then we went to various dental offices including the Special Needs Clinic. They couldn't do anything with Abie. They wanted to put Abie out with anesthesia every two years for a cleaning, x-rays, and any dental treatment he might need. Anesthesia is extreme for just a dental cleaning. Plus it carries a risk.

I finally found a dentist who said he could handle Abie without anesthesia. First, I held Abie in the dental chair while he held him in a headlock and worked on him. Then as he got bigger, Jon came with me. When Jon and I couldn't hold him down anymore, we called the Department of Mental Retardation. They sent somebody to help. She helped us restrain him at the dentist.

However, recently, she said it was cruel to hold him down like that. "He's afraid of the dentist. It would be better to work on reducing his fear of the dentist, not on exacerbating his fear," she said.

Dr. Treisman asked, "What do you think?"

"I think she's right. There's no way we can go on like this. We need to reduce Abie's fear of the dentist. We need to work on this in a systematic way rather than forcing him."

"Is the school doing anything to help you with this?"

"No, not at all. They said they don't work on that. Their advice was to put him out with anesthesia every two years. They assured me that many of their students had dental care this way. Many students at the Behavioral School have teeth missing by the time they graduate at age 22. I don't want that for Abie. This is what I think happens when you ignore dental care for two years at a time. Besides, Abie's communication skills are still so poor. I want to make sure he doesn't have a toothache without us knowing about it. This business of putting him out every two years puts him at risk for that."

"How is Abie's communication doing?"

"I would say the same. No improvement. He has his soft inarticulate words which they ignore, and he hates using the communication book."

"What about behaviors?"

"He has tantrums and some self-injurious behavior. He bites his wrist." Then I showed Dr. Treisman the bites on his wrist.

"Okay. You need some help. You need someone to help you with the dental piece, the communication, and the behaviors."

"I'm afraid that the school isn't really helping with these things."

"Is there another school you think could help?"

"Well, the New Progress School rejected Abie about a year ago. At that time, I looked other private programs, but their wait lists were long. It didn't even pay to look at them. I also tried the public school, but that didn't work out either."

"Then you need help after school and on weekends."

"Oh yes, I certainly do."

"There's state money available for children like Abie who are at risk for a residential placement because of autism or intellectual disability." She had a piece of paper that described eligibility requirements. The paper read as follows:

Eligibility Requirements for Flexible Intensive Services
Recipients must:
1. Have a severe disability that affects many aspects of daily life.
2. Require 24/7 education to generalize skills.
3. Be currently living at home with family.

4. Have a family member willing to spend time running the program.
5. Be between the ages of 10 and 16.
6. Be in danger of being placed residentially.
7. Be currently underserved and in need of additional services.

"The Department of Mental Retardation runs the program, but it is funded jointly with the Department of Education. They created the program to address situations just like yours. In flexible intensive services, you get to decide what you work on. My evaluation, which I will mail you next week, will outline Abie's needs as we have discussed. Abie needs 24/7 intervention. He needs a comprehensive home program. That will help him improve."

I was losing steam with working with Abie. I clearly needed help, and this seemed like just what we needed. At last, instead of doing all of the work myself, I could get helpers… not just a few hours a month, but something like twenty hours a week. My hope was beginning to return as I thought about Abie receiving help from Maureen Pauley twenty hours a week. That would make up for his school situation. He would improve so much with help like this.

Keeping Abie out of a residential placement was a very worthy goal. His chance of living independently was probably not in the cards, but maybe at least I might be able to get him to the point that he could continue to live with Jon and me when he got older.

I called the Department of Mental Retardation the moment I got home. The service coordinator, Corrine Marks, took down the information and told me Abie would go on a waiting list. She didn't ask to visit us or anything. It was all too easy. I was ecstatic, and for the next six months, I watched the telephone while I tried to will it to ring. I heard nothing. After three more months, I called Corrine back to check to see where he was on the wait list. Corrine said they had families who were in crisis. These families needed the service more than we did, but Abie was still on the wait list. She'd contact us when our names came up.

Someone from my online support group told me Darlene Diamond had flexible intensive services for Matt for a few years already. He was one of the first recipients of this service. Someone else told me a family whose high functioning autistic child wanted driving lessons got the service. While each person's circumstances are different, this made no sense to me.

After the popular book, *Let Me Hear Your Voice*, by Catherine Maurice was published, there emerged recognition in the disability community that children diagnosed with autism needed home programming. Gradually a few providers of home based services began to appear, but many of them were plagued with workforce issues. Autism families were underserved, and more and more parents were fighting for long-term home programming through the schools and through flexible intensive services.

I wondered what was holding up the process for flexible intensive services for Abie. We were on the wait list for ten months with no word. I called Corrine Marks once again, but she had left the Department of Mental Retardation for another job. I asked to speak to someone else regarding flexible intensive services. They referred me to Katie Norsbeth.

Katie didn't return my phone calls, but I was very persistent. I called her every day once a day for two weeks. I figured she might be on vacation. So I skipped a week and called her once a day for another two weeks. Finally as I was about to call her in the third week, she called me back. She said, "I'm not sure why you keep calling me. I don't see your son's name here on the wait list for flexible intensive services. You haven't gone through the application process."

My heart beat faster. "How can that be? I spoke to Corrine Marks, and she said that I was on the wait list. I kept following up. She assured me that Abie's name would come up eventually. Were we waiting for nothing?" My voice started to crack as the tears rolled from my eyes. *Why did it have to be this way? Why did we have to fight for every crumb? This program was geared precisely towards us. Why couldn't we just get it? What was I doing wrong?*

"Corrine is no longer working for us, but she wouldn't have just put you on a wait list. You needed to be accepted into the program to go on the wait list. You must have misunderstood. We work very closely with the school systems around the state. Your school system didn't recommend your son for flexible intensive services. I just called Mary Carpenter to confirm this, and she was under the same impression that I was."

"But my son fits into the program like a hand in glove. Why didn't the school system recommend him? Wouldn't we be entitled to these services?"

"I don't know why the school didn't recommend your son. He probably wasn't as needy as some of the other students. Our program is not an entitlement like the free and appropriate education the school must provide. We have many deserving and needy families we need to serve. We cannot serve just anybody. I'm afraid we cannot offer you services or have you on our wait list at this time."

The flexible intensive services program was not an entitlement, but free and appropriate education was. At that point, I had received training as a special education advocate at the state's Parent Training and Information Center. I had a better idea of what my rights were. I had a piece of paper in hand from Dr. Treisman. It said Abie needed 24/7 education. I was in a good position to fight for home programming from the school system. It was time to take action, and turn the situation around.

I called Mary Carpenter the next day. I told her Abie needed 24/7 education which included a home-based program. I told her I was going to reject the IEP in part because we needed more services from the school district.

In order to fight the school district for additional services, I had to reject the IEP in part. The Behavioral School said many times they would kick Abie out of the school if we ever rejected an IEP they wrote. I was nervous to tell Patricia Stone I was going to reject the IEP in part.

My voice was shaky as I spoke to Patricia on the phone. "I just wanted to discuss a few things with you. First I want to tell you what a wonderful job you're doing with Abie. I'm just so grateful."

"Of course, that's what all our parents say."

They'd better say that or else…"The school is doing a fabulous job, just fabulous!" I said.

"Thanks. I appreciate your calling to tell me that."

"Abie is making so many gains at the school, but we need help at home to help him generalize all these skills to the home setting. So we're fighting for some home programming from the school district." Okay… it was false flattery and not exactly true. But what else could I say?

"Many of our students are getting flexible intensive services from the DMR. Some have also approached us about doing home programs for older students. We've decided not to offer this service. We're not certain we could benefit financially from it. I don't know where you'd go to get decent services, but I think you should consider applying for flexible intensive services from the DMR rather than fighting the school district for services," said Patricia.

"I agree with you. I already applied for flexible intensive services, but Abie was rejected."

"REJECTED! Based on what? There are children who aren't nearly as needy as Abie who are getting these services. That doesn't make sense. "

Patricia sounded indignant when she said those words, and it occurred to me that she saw herself as an advocate for kids with disabilities. "No, it doesn't make sense, so I'm trying to get the services through the school district. I just wanted you to know that I'm rejecting the IEP to fight for home services. It has nothing to do with the services we receive from the Behavioral School. When I reject the IEP, your team doesn't necessarily have to be at the meeting if you don't want to come."

"We wouldn't want to. It would probably be best if we stayed out of it, but good luck."

"Thank you, Patricia." I felt grateful and relieved. She wasn't going to stand in my way. I anticipated her telling me the Behavioral School provided everything we needed and we didn't need other services. For some unknown reason, she didn't say that. *Maybe things could possibly get better at the school. She was on my side.* The last time I felt grateful to her was when she accepted Abie into the school. Perhaps there was even more to be hopeful about.

The next day I sent a letter to Mary Carpenter. It said I was partially rejecting the IEP because we needed home programming. I referred to the neurologist's report, and sent a copy along with the letter. I sent the letter certified mail, return receipt requested. When I received the green returned receipt, I called Mary Carpenter.

"Hello, this is Arlene Dancer. You must have received my letter partially rejecting the IEP."

"No, I don't think so. I didn't receive anything like that."

"I sent a letter partially rejecting the IEP because we need home based services. I am requesting an emergency team meeting."

"I don't know what you are talking about, and I'm shocked. You're receiving such wonderful… and I might add… very expensive services at the Behavioral School. We aren't responsible for engaging your son every minute of every day. You aren't working. You need to take care of your own child. We're providing appropriate schooling. This is not our responsibility."

"We need an emergency IEP team meeting."

"I don't think so. You're receiving high-priced services the public schools are paying for. That's my final word. No meeting. It's not necessary."

"Okay. Are you sure about that?"

"Oh, yes."

The next day I filed a complaint with the Department of Education Program Quality and Assurance. I sent them copies of my letter, the signed return receipt, and a copy of Dr. Treisman's report. Two days later, I received a call from Mary Carpenter. She wanted to meet with me alone. She said it wasn't necessary to have a complete IEP team meeting. I agreed with her. We met in her office.

"Abie needs home programming," I said.

"Home programming is a problem for the school system. What happens if we send someone to your home, and Abie has an aggression, and the person gets hurt? We could be sued."

"Not my problem."

"Okay. Listen… I'm going to help. The Department of Mental Retardation has a program called flexible intensive services. The Department of Education partially subsidizes the program, and the school districts work very closely with the DMR to identify those students who might be in need of these services. Abie qualifies to be in that program. I might be able to persuade the folks over at the DMR that he should be on their wait list. That program is very flexible. You can get exactly what you think you need."

"Yes, I know about that program, but for some reason, they said we can't get services."

"I'm in a position to help you get those services."

"Great. I still want to continue to try to get home based services from the school district."

"It's not our responsibility. The DMR can take care of it."

"Is that a 'no'? I need notification on why you can't provide services that have been recommended by Abie's neurologist, Dr. Doris Treisman. If you don't provide us with a written reason why the school cannot provide what Dr. Treisman recommended, I'll place another complaint with the DOE."

"It's a 'no' when it comes to providing home programming from the school, but I'm going to get you more than the home programming you are seeking...... through the DMR flexible intensive services. That way you'll get more than what you want, and it won't strain the school budgets. The flexible intensive services program will get you home programming, materials, respite, flexible funding, everything. Don't go to the Department of Education. I'm going to write out that notification today and drop it in the mail."

Three days later, I received the notification on why the Newtucktin school district wouldn't provide the home programming the neurologist recommended. The notification said the DMR should be providing the services through flexible intensive services, and home programming was not the school's responsibility. I knew this particular reason did not let the schools off the hook. The argument would not hold up at a due process hearing. On the afternoon of the day I received the notification, Katie Norsbeth from the DMR called me.

"I've been speaking with Mary Carpenter. The Newtucktin School District meant to sign off on flexible intensive services programming for your son, Abie. It was an oversight that he wasn't placed on the wait list. I'm going to put him on the wait list today. We're so sorry about this mistake."

"How long do you expect the wait to be?"

"About eight months to a year."

"We've already waited almost a year. He needs programming NOW."

"We can't provide that now. There are families who were on the list before you."

"Were the families told they were on the list when they weren't... like us?"

"I don't know what Corrine did. I don't have any documentation of it. I only have your story. The best I can do is to put you on the end of the list. I'm sorry."

"Okay. It is what it is. I'm glad that he's on the list now. What are the next steps?"

"I'll send someone out to talk to you about flexible intensive services, but it's just a formality....because I am putting you on the list today. I'll call you next week about that."

"Corrine said Abie was on the wait list before when apparently we weren't. How do I know that he is actually on the list now?"

"Well, you'll just have to trust me. I'm sorry this happened, but there's nothing I can do about it."

After I spoke to Katie Norsbeth from the DMR, I immediately sent the Bureau of Special Education Appeals a letter initiating a due process hearing with the school. I was determined that Abie was going to get home programming, not just a promise of a wait list. I figured we waited long enough. It was time to take action.

Mary Carpenter called me the next week. "Why did you initiate a due process hearing? I arranged it so Abie could receive flexible intensive services. You don't need programming from the school. That would be redundant services."

"The DMR offered me a wait list, not home programming. Therefore, I am going to pursue home programming from the school district."

"But why? I thought we had a good relationship. I told the DMR that Abie should get the flexible intensive services even though you were already receiving very expensive school services. Isn't that enough? Do you have to take revenge and hold a grudge? Why are you doing this to me?"

"This is nothing personal. Abie needs these services. He's needed these services for years, but I delayed fighting for them properly. Now I'm ready. This isn't about you. It's about him, and his needs. "

"Who is your lawyer? That Leila Fine?"

"I haven't decided yet, but I did decide I'm going through with the due process hearing. I want these services for Abie, and I'll do the absolute best I can to fight for him."

"I think you are making a mistake."

"I don't."

"Okay, I see that we are getting nowhere. Maybe you ought to think about it. You can always cancel the hearing. You can do this even the last minute."

I decided to go to hearing without an expensive lawyer. I was a trained advocate, and I knew what I was doing. I had my papers, and I was prepared. I waited with anticipation for the date of the pre-hearing. Many disputes get resolved at the pre-hearing conference, but even more disputes get resolved as the pre-hearing date approaches. The day before the date of the pre-hearing conference, Mary Carpenter called me. "We're prepared to contract with PCPP Educational Services to provide home programming to Abie. We can provide ten hours of home programming."

I had never heard of PCPP Educational Services, but I hoped they were a good. "We're seeking twenty hours of home programming," I replied.

"Would you agree to ten hours?"

I thought about it for a minute. We weren't receiving any home programming at the time. *Maybe it would be best to take the offer, and get something going right away.* I really didn't want to have a long drawn out fight with the school system. I also thought the flexible intensive services programming from the DMR might eventually come through.

"Would PCPP Educational Services be willing to hire our respite worker as Abie's home therapist?"

"Is she qualified?"

"Yes, she's certified in severe special needs, has a master's, and she works at the Behavioral School."

"I don't see why not. They would probably be happy to hire someone like that."

The thought of having help from Maureen Pauley filled my heart with joy and anticipation. *Yes, this would be good.* "Okay. We'll accept the ten hours a week. When will this start?"

"I'll call them and tell them you have accepted our offer. Then they'll call and set up an appointment with you and Abie. Will you cancel the due process hearing?"

"Yes, I will... once I see the updated service grid on the IEP."

I was surprised when I heard Mary Carpenter say, "good luck

with the home program."

"Thanks. I can't wait for this to start. I am so hopeful this will help Abie."

After I signed the updated IEP, I called the Bureau of Special Education Appeals. Then I fantasized about the jump in learning that Abie would have by spending that amount of time with Maureen Pauley. Ten hours a week!

Three days after I called off the hearing, Maureen Pauley called me to tell me she was getting married to her fiancé. He took a job in Minnesota. They were going to get married, move there, and start their own family. She wouldn't be able to provide respite anymore. I never got a chance to ask her to work in our home program. It was too late. She was leaving, and I wished her well. She deserved her happiness. I was grateful for what she gave us. I appreciated having known her, not just because of what she taught Abie, but also for helping me keep my faith in human beings and their capacity for goodness. I would have been in some sorry state if not for people like her.

Craig Miller from PCPP Educational Services called me the following week. He wanted to assess what our needs were. I liked Craig, and so did Abie. He seemed to have a way with Abie. The ability to work with a kid like Abie is a skill that not too many people have. However, having that skill doesn't necessarily mean you also have the skills needed to organize a program.

Two weeks later Katie Norsbeth called. Our names had come up on the list for flexible intensive services. I expected to be waiting eight months to a year, but something had changed. Katie gave me the names of three providers. She arranged appointments with all three to come to our house. One of the providers was PCPP Educational Services, and they were already familiar with us.

I had my pick of the three providers, but with Maureen Pauley leaving for Minnesota, I chose PCPP Educational Services.

PCPP Educational Services was going to take 33 percent of the flexible intensive services money, but in return, they promised to provide trained ABA therapists and an expert ABA consultant for our program. Since we already had a contract with them through the schools, they seemed like the best choice. I didn't want the hassle of hiring and training staff, and I certainly didn't want the hassle of working with more than one agency.

The other proposed providers were offering "assistance" with the flexible intensive services grant, but they were not going to hire and train people to work in a home program. Their fees were 20 percent of the grant, but it wasn't clear what services they provided. The only service they committed themselves to was to conduct background checks and payroll. The people working in the home program were independent contractors, so the payroll wasn't that complicated. They didn't need to pay taxes or take out money for benefits for these employees.

Chapter 13: The Dentist

Arlene's Thoughts

I had the flexible intensive services grant, and I was going to get additional hours of ABA therapy from the school system. Help was finally on the way. Infused with new energy, I was ready to work on Abie's most difficult problem, his issues at the dentist. According to conventional thought, we were trying to do the impossible. Dental treatment for Abie without general anesthesia was supposed to be impossible. Several dentists we visited were certain of that. Dental treatment under general anesthesia once every two years was the accepted gold standard for individuals like Abie. I didn't want to argue about conventional standard with anyone. I just wanted to help my son.

My friend, Annette Levine, was a dentist. She never worked with an autistic patient, but she was willing to help Abie and me. She offered to help us free of charge, but this was going to involve hard work and a lot of time. It would take her away from her other patients and her own large family. We needed to pay her for this work.

Annette didn't believe dental care under anesthesia was the best idea for a child or adult with a severe developmental disability. She was somewhat of a maverick. She believed an awful lot could happen if you left dental care undone for so long. Anesthesia carried risks. If there were another way, she believed we should take that. She was the right person for this job. We were on the exact same wave length.

Abie needed a behavioral dental desensitization program. This was going to require many visits. Dental insurance only paid for two visits per year. He was going to need as many visits as possible to get him willing to accept dental treatment. We settled on once a week to start. The flexible intensive services grant paid for the additional visits. We were on our way. My advocacy paid off. Better days were ahead.

Abie's Thoughts

Flexible intensive services…those words made Mommy happy. For a long time, she was not as much fun as she used to be. Sometimes she got very angry with the bosses in my school. She was also mad at Mary Carpenter and a person named DMR. When she was mad, I felt bad. Therefore, I wanted to block out the world by doing self-stimulatory behavior.

After we got flexible intensive services, I never had to see Dr. Mooney, the dentist, anymore. I hated Dr. Mooney. He was meaner than Shere Kahn, the tiger who wanted to eat Mowgli. Dr. Mooney used to grab a hold of my neck, squeeze it tight, and then he tortured me by putting sharp knives and pokers into my teeth. Mommy, Daddy, and another lady held me down so he could do this awful thing to me. Sometimes Mommy cried when he was doing this. I don't understand why they held me down while that terrible man did terrible things to me. I still believed Mommy wanted to help and protect me, but somehow she didn't know that this was bad.

Anyway, now I go to Dr. Levine instead. I watch Mary Poppins, and I have a good time there instead of being tortured.

Dr. Levine has a torture room just like Dr. Mooney. I was afraid to go in there too. Instead of holding me down, Dr. Levine played a movie in her room. The movie stayed on when I sat in the chair. The movie went off if I left the chair. She didn't grab my neck, and nobody held me down. We visited Dr. Levine every week back then. I was her favorite patient. Little by little I learned to accept dental care. This was impossible because a PDD low functioning autistic retard cannot do dental care. I heard them say that at many dental torture rooms. Instead of doing dental care, retards like me lose our teeth, and get many toothaches. Mommy doesn't like that, and neither does Dr. Levine. So we did the impossible. The impossible is something that can't be done because it is not possible. It doesn't make sense when you do the impossible because if you do it, it's possible. This is something like a clever retard. No retard is clever, but yet some of us are. Maybe all of us are, and the real people are the ones who aren't clever. Nobody really knows.

When I first went to Dr. Levine, she had to remove all of her stimmy plants because I'd touch them. Gradually she put them back in. She told me I was a good boy for not touching them. She thought I was good. I liked that.

At my first visit with Dr. Levine, she didn't wear her dentist outfit called "scrubs." She wanted to fool me and make me think she wasn't a dentist. I knew she was a dentist anyway. Whenever someone's first name is "doctor," they're going to touch you and poke you. I was already twelve years old so I knew this. Even a PDD low functioning uneducable autistic retard knows this. She had a torture room just like the other dentists, so she couldn't fool me by wearing her regular clothes.

I didn't want to go into Dr. Levine's dental torture room, but she played Mary Poppins on the TV. I wanted to watch that.

She enticed me. "Come in and watch the movie. It's Mary Poppins. I heard you like Mary Poppins."

I wanted no part of the dental torture room, so I walked away. When I walked away, Mary Poppins stopped playing on the TV. So then, I tried going back into the room. Mary Poppins started playing again.

Dr. Levine said, "Abie, you can relax in the chair and watch the movie. You'll be more comfortable that way. Put your head in that little pillow. It is really comfy. All my patients like it."

So I took the risk and sat in the chair. But when I sat in that chair, I saw that she had scratchers, pokers, and weird obnoxious sound makers, just like Dr. Mooney. I didn't want any part of that, so I got out of the chair, and went out of the room. Once I was out of the chair, Mary Poppins stopped playing. So that was the deal. If I stayed in the chair, Mary Poppins played. If I got up, Mary Poppins stopped. For a few visits, I only had to sit in the chair and watch the movie. After a few weeks, I had to open my mouth to get to watch the movie. After a few months, I had to let Dr. Levine insert instruments in my mouth to get to watch the movie. After several months, I had to bite down on the x-ray film in order to get to watch the movie. After a long time and many visits, I found myself sitting there while Dr. Levine took x-rays and cleaned and checked my teeth.

Whenever Dr. Levine used a poker, a scratcher, or an obnoxious noisemaker, she explained to me why she had to do that. She said I had plaque on my teeth. She needed to use the poker and the scratcher to clean off the plaque and make my mouth all clean and tidy. Mommy and Daddy told me all about ten plaques on Passover. They sounded bad, even worse than the wicked witch melting down. Frogs jumping around all over the place, water in swimming pools that turned into blood, and locusts, which are bad insects like mosquitoes. I wondered how all of that got into my mouth, but I was glad that Dr. Levine was able to scrap that away with her scratcher.

I didn't understand Dr. Levine's explanations of why she did what she did. I understood she was saying nice things to make me not scared anymore. She was my friend, and she liked me a lot.

Dr. Levine said I'm her most improved patient. Also I'm her absolute favorite patient. Out of all of the people who sit in her dental chair, I am the most important. Think about that... a **PDD** low functioning autistic retard... and I am the best and the most important!

Chapter 14: A Step Forward

Arlene's Thoughts

J ust around the time that we finally received flexible intensive services, I learned that an organized comprehensive system for teaching language actually did exist.

Some mothers on my online support group recommended that I go to some conferences on verbal behavior.

At the time I attended these conferences, Abie was already twelve years old... way past the magic age of five.

Verbal behavior is based on the book, *Verbal Behavior* by B.F. Skinner. Skinner analyzed how language developed in human beings in this book. Linguist, Noam Chomsky, who believes the development of language is innate, sharply refuted Skinner's book. So who was correct about the origins of language? Was it Skinner or was it Chomsky? I certainly didn't care. I was just a mom trying to help her kid.

For those who do not develop language, using Skinner's observations to facilitate the development of speech and language made much more sense to me than having no systematic plan for developing language. Some ABA professionals don't know about verbal behavior because not all colleges and universities teach it.

During one conference, the speaker showed us some videos of children having trouble communicating with their given system. He explained what was going on, and how to make it better.

Intervention based on verbal behavior motivates a child, adolescent or adult to learn language by connecting words with their purposes.

I learned that sign language might be beneficial for those who had no oral speech or for those whose oral speech was difficult to understand. Your hands are always with you. You decide what you want to say immediately. Signing could be more reinforcing for some learners than picture communication because it can be faster. It might get you to your reward sooner. There was no such thing as iPads at that time. In those days, a picture system meant turning through pages, and scanning many pictures.

I learned about the various functions of language. I was on the edge of my seat as I devoured every word that the speaker said. Everything he said rang true.

During the break, I went up to him to ask a question. "My son has a habit of biting his wrist. I know that it's difficult to give me advice when you've never met him, but what could be some possible reasons for this type of behavior?"

"Does he try to communicate that he wants something after the bite?"

I thought about it for a minute. "Yes, he usually does."

"Is he in a large classroom with many children with behaviors in it?"

"Yes. That's right."

"Most likely the shock value of the bite is enough to grab someone's attention in the classroom. Then he can make his request."

"Sounds right. What do I do?"

"If you want to get rid of it, only honor requests that are not preceded by the bite. Help him to do the request without the bite."

While the answer was obvious, it was never obvious to those who were working with Abie at the school. I knew the school didn't allow parents to suggest any ways to help their children at the school. So I kept quiet and only worked on getting rid of these bites at home.

After that conference, I knew I wanted a verbal behavior program for Abie. I wanted him to have what he should have had when he was two years old. It was late, but at least he would get it. I arranged for Craig Miller to join me at other verbal behavior conferences. I told him I wanted staff in our home program who were either trained in verbal behavior or willing to receive training in verbal behavior.

Our verbal behavior speaker wanted us to bring in videotapes of a therapist or of ourselves working with our children for his next conference. He was going to comment on them one by one. I was so proud of my video. My many years of experience of working with Abie showed through in that video. He got all of the answers right. I was sure he would use my video as an example to the others on how to do things correctly.

It finally came my time for my critique. Everyone watched silently. Then he said, "You really have a lovely dining room. I like the chairs. But your teaching technique could be improved."

"Abie's getting all of the answers right. How can that be improved?"

"I'm not overly concerned about correct answers. I'm more concerned about his interest in learning. He looks like he's bored and not very happy. You have to make this much more interesting so he wants to come back for more."

"That's the general problem. He doesn't like learning. He only does it for the reward."

"Then give him more rewards."

"More food rewards?"

"No, step up the pace. The reward is the next activity. The quicker the pace the quicker he gets to his reward. That will make it more interesting.'

I was confused. "Much faster? He needs the time to process the information."

"Says who?"

"Everyone says this… I mean the professionals say this."

"Based on what?"

"I don't know what they base it on, but they all say it. I don't see how another activity can be a reward."

"It's a reward because it gets him closer to his ultimate goal… which is the food reward or stimmer. It's reinforcing."

"Are you sure about this?" I asked incredulously.

"Listen, sometimes when somebody doesn't really know something, they make things up. Then one person hears it from another until many people think there is something to it. There's no evidence that providing extra time for processing information helps kids on the spectrum. I don't know of any study to date that proves this. However, we know reinforcement works. Step up the pace. Do whatever you can to make your instruction more interesting. If he likes videotapes, use them as rewards, stop the videotape and do some intensive teaching while the video is stopped. Remember HE has to choose to sit and learn with you. If you don't make your instruction interesting enough, he can make the choice of just stimming….. and you don't want that."

"Okay…it's time to change my way of instruction and step up the pace."

Abie's Thoughts

Up until I was about twelve years old, Mommy used to teach me by talking very slowly and then asking me boring stuff.

"Point…. to… toothbrush…. good job, Abie….

you…. pointed… to… toothbrush."

Now "point….. to…. cra…cker."

Real people talk this special way to retards. They do this because they think we're slow thinkers and very stupid. The teachers and bosses told Mommy this over and over again, and she believed them. I can't stand this kind of talk, and I want to stim to block it out.

Mommy went to some conferences, and started doing things differently. She stopped talking in retard- speak, and talked normally. I liked this.

She had a huge stack of pictures, and very quickly she would say things like:

"The one that you use to clean teeth is a………." then I said "toothbrush" and pointed to the picture of the toothbrush.

"You eat………." Then I said "cracker" and pointed to the cracker.

"Show me the one that can have hot water and soap in it," Then I pointed to bathtub.

What do you do with a fork? Then I tried to say "eat."

While I enjoyed this more than the old discrete trials, I already knew many words. It was during these sessions that I finally realized that everything in the world had a name, every action had a name, and people communicated with each other using these names. I watched my Disney movies, and I realized more of what was happening.

We also did something called "manding sessions." This meant I got the chance to ask for many things. When I had speech therapy, we did similar exercises, but manding exercises were different because everything I requested were things I actually liked…..like tiny pieces of my favorite food or a period of time I could have a stimmer. Also, in speech therapy, the speech therapist did most of the talking. In a manding session, I did the talking. Both my talking and communicating and my understanding of language increased after these changes to my sessions with Mommy. I also enjoyed learning much more. For the first time in a long time, I was less interested in blocking out the world in my sessions with Mommy. I liked figuring out what the world had to offer. This made up for not seeing Maureen any more. She went to some place where they have mini sodas. Maybe she got them at vending machines. She was my favorite, and I wished that I could see her smiling face again.

In school whenever we tried to learn something, it was very slow and boring. I couldn't stand it so I tuned it out. It became very different from the teaching at home. Mommy tried to get my teachers to do things the way I liked, but it was no use. They wanted to do what they always did.

Chapter 15: The Home Program

Arlene's Thoughts

Whenever we tried to help Abie, there was always a road blocker to prevent us from doing so. It had been three months since the school district gave us the go ahead to start our program, but PCPP Educational Services still didn't hire anyone to work in Abie's home program. We had the funding for the home program, but nobody to work in it.

According to the law, the school system was obligated to provide home programming services because the service grid of the IEP listed these services. In addition, if we didn't use up the money in the flexible intensive services grant, we had to return the funding back to the state at the end of the fiscal year. We were spending only a small fraction of the flexible intensive services money on additional dental visits. We didn't use any of the rest of the money because we had no staffing.

I was still doing all of the ABA home therapy. With Maureen Pauley gone, I didn't even have the five hours of respite. Abie's school day flew while I attended to everything. He still needed 24/7 attention. I couldn't do things like throw in a laundry or do shopping when he was around. I had to do all of those things while he was in school. I even made the dinner before he got home, and I warmed it up just before we ate. When he got home, he needed my complete attention. It was like having a two year old in a twelve-year-old body.

I called Craig Miller every chance I got. "Craig, it's been three months. What's holding up our program?"

"Verbal behavior isn't popular. It's hard to find people who want to get into it."

"Remember they don't have to be trained in VB. I'll send them to training. They just have to be willing to use the method. Listen, if you cannot find any VB people; just send me whoever you have. I'll try to convince them to use the VB."

"In that case, I do have a possible consultant for your program."

The consultant's job was to train the home therapists, and help with the design of the programming.

"The consultant's name is Bev. She worked for the New Progress School for ten years. She has a master's in applied behavior analysis. Do you want to meet her?" asked Craig.

"Absolutely. Let's set up an appointment for her to meet Abie."

Bev and Craig arrived the following Thursday just as Abie was getting off the van. Both of them greeted Abie. They immediately tried to engage him. I was impressed.

I asked Bev, "I was thinking about placing Abie in the New Progress School at one time, but it didn't work out. I noticed they weren't too flexible in terms of their programming. Did you notice that when you worked there?"

"Many parents complained about that. There was one parent who was livid and caused a lot of trouble when she found out we had given her child Ipecac."

"Ipecac?"

"Yeah, we gave the kids Ipecac whenever we made a medication mistake. The Ipecac would correct the issue by making the child vomit. Anyway, the mom had to bring the child to the emergency room for another reason. So we had to tell her we Ipecaced her son earlier in the day. She was so mad."

"Wait a minute. When the New Progress School gives a child Ipecac, they don't tell the parents?"

"Oh no, of course not! Not when I was working there... not unless we had to for some medical reason. Telling the parents would only upset them... so why do that?"

"Don't they have a right to know?"

"No, there's nothing in any regulation that gives parents the right to know. New Progress has them sign a waiver to consent to first aid. It covers this."

A red flag was waving, but Bev was engaging Abie. I didn't know what to think. "Bev, we want to do a verbal behavior program here. We'll train you in the method. Is that a problem for you?"

"It isn't really a problem for me, but why do you want to use an unproven method when we have proven scientific methods readily available?"

"Verbal behavior is ABA for the development of language. It's been proven just as much as any other ABA."

"While I disagree, I'd be willing to learn more about it."

I was leery about her answer, but I changed the subject. "We haven't hired any direct service people yet, so there's nobody to train yet. We're going to hire people to work from 4 pm until 9 pm and on weekends. Are you available during those times to train our direct service workers?"

"I have kids, so I wouldn't be able to work at all during any of those times. I quit my job at the New Progress School so I'd have time to spend with my kids. I don't want to leave them to work in the evening. I only want to work while they're in school... mothers' hours."

Craig interjected, "We thought we could arrange once a month meetings with your therapists during the day. Bev could train during those meetings, and we could troubleshoot problems."

"Bev wouldn't actually get a chance to see the therapists working with Abie."

"You could videotape the sessions," answered Craig.

"No, I need someone who's going to sit by the therapists and actually show them how to do it. I don't think this is going to work. I am sorry, Bev."

The following day Craig Miller called me. "You should reconsider Bev. Did you like her?"

"She had some positive qualities, but I want someone who's willing to work in the trenches with the therapists, not someone who's just giving orders. I need someone who's going to troubleshoot in real time. She isn't it. Besides, if the hours of the therapists are from 4 to 9, it may be difficult for them to make a meeting during the day. I'm going to say "no" on hiring Bev."

"Okay, that's your prerogative."

Three more months went by. No therapists and no consultant.

I found out about a consultant that other people in Newtucktin were using. Her name was Susan, and she was open to verbal behavior. She already had some verbal behavior training, and was interested in working in our program.

I called Craig Miller. "I found a consultant for our home program. Can PCPP Educational Services put her on the payroll?"

"That's wonderful. Of course, we'll have to check out her resume and run a background check. If she checks out, we'd be happy to put her on the payroll."

"Since I found the person, and your agency could not, how much of a percentage will the agency be taking from the grant?"

"The agency's cut is 33 percent whether you find the people or whether we find the people. It makes no difference."

That hardly seemed fair to me. "It's been more than six months, and you have yet to send even one prospect for a therapist."

"Six months? Really? Has it been that long? We did place an ad in the paper last week."

"LAST WEEK! You should've placed ads six months ago. "

"The Newtucktin school system phoned me and told me you placed a complaint. Your complaint said they were in non-compliance with the IEP because you don't have a home therapist for Abie."

"Yes, that's right. It's been six months. How long do you expect me to wait?"

"I have a person for you. She is a Russian immigrant, and her name in Anya. She's very good. You'll really like her."

I was shocked. I figured that PCPP would never hire anyone for us. "You do?"

"Yes, I do. I could send her to you tomorrow."

"Can she work twenty or thirty hours?"

"No, I've given her other clients. She just asked for more hours."

"Okay. I also placed a job posting at the university. Several students responded. I may hire one or more of them as well."

"Well, you see… everything does seem to be working out. These things take a while. It looks like your home program is shaping up."

I met Anya the following day. She was able to work with Abie. She was terrific, but she could only work two days a week. I was happy to hire her.

I also found a student who had previously worked in a Lovaas program. Her name was Jessy. She was open to verbal behavior and really seemed to like Abie. She was from California, and seemed quite homesick for her family.

I couldn't arrange for Jessy to go to a verbal behavior workshop because of her schedule. Instead we were going to work together for a while until she got the hang of it. Anya, however, had a more flexible schedule, and was able to go to the workshop.

I felt more hopeful than ever. We assembled a great team. This was the intervention every kid with autism should have. For every dollar the DMR gave us for intensive services, PCPP took a third of the money. They did get us Anya. They also did background checks on our workers and they cut checks. I managed the program and scheduled the staff.

Abie's Thoughts

Mommy no longer cared whether I was willing point to a coat for no reason. But she did want me to know I'm supposed to wear a coat when the weather gets cold." Sometimes she said, "Let's go outside. It's cold outside. Get ready." Then I was supposed to get my coat. If didn't get my coat, she said "coat" to give me a hint. I was tired of "point to coat, point to cup, point to elephant." I hoped the teachers in school would stop asking me to "point to this, point to that," but they kept on asking anyway. It made me bored. It made me mad. It made me want to stim and block out the entire world. When was it ever going to end?

I had a good time with Mommy after school and on weekends. Anyway, she spoiled our good time by having all sorts of new teachers come to our house. I didn't want the new teachers. I wanted Mommy and Daddy. New teachers didn't understand me. The ones at school thought I was stupid. I heard it all the time in school..."Abie doesn't understand this. Abie can't do that." I understood just fine. I didn't want to do what they wanted me to. They didn't believe in me, so I didn't believe in them. Mommy was always saying she was tired and needed a break. So she hired Susan, Anya, and Jessy. They did flexible intensive services. I don't know what that is.

Mommy still worked with me with Dr. Levine and on other things. She spent a lot of time getting teaching sessions ready for me, and making sure I had the right materials. She also had some green paper with many squares on them. She drew lines that went up and down called "graphs" on those pieces of paper. She talked to Susan about them. This had something to do with the data samples. Data samples have nothing to do with the samples they give you in the supermarket so don't get excited over nothing.

Mommy talked to Anya and Jessy about me, and many times sat in on our sessions. Sometimes she took videotapes of us, and watched us over and over again. Whenever a therapist didn't show up, Mommy would fill in. She kept asking me to speak louder. She touched my throat so I would know where the voice was supposed to come from. I usually spoke in a whisper, but if I tried hard, I could have a loud voice. When I made stim noises, these always came out loud. Sometimes they came out as a scream, but I never had any control over these. They just happened.

I began to notice our house had all its things in the right places after I got my new home teachers. Also, Mommy smiled a lot more.

After a while, I did like Anya, and Jessy. Both Anya and Jessy knew I was smart and understood many things. But Susan didn't know I understood what she said.

Susan said, "Abie doesn't understand the videos he watches. He's just interested in the motion and colors." Jessy knew she was wrong, but Susan was the boss.

After about a year of working with Susan, she told Mommy that I should have smaller food rewards. "Just cut up the pieces smaller."

Mommy didn't think I would be happy with smaller rewards. "Abie's going to be angry if we do that. He'll probably tantrum."

"Oh, no he won't even notice the difference. It's fine," Susan replied.

"I can't have Anya or Jessy give him the smaller rewards. He'll tantrum, and might have an aggression. I don't want either of them to get hurt."

"Don't be ridiculous. He won't have an aggression over that. When we hand him the reward, we'll be reinforcing him. He'll love it. I swear to you he doesn't know the difference."

When I heard those words, I got angry. Mommy was looking at my face. Both Anya and Jessy were there also, and they were looking at me.

Then Mommy said to Susan, "I'd be willing to try this if YOU were to use the smaller food rewards. Then if it works out okay, we can have Anya and Jessy take over."

"Okay. I'd be willing to do that, but it's totally unnecessary," Susan said.

"Yes, I'd appreciate if you did it first." Mommy had little pieces of steak to give me for a reward. She cut these very small. She took the small pieces and cut them even smaller. Then Susan came to the table. I hated her and didn't want her to sit next to me, but I waited.

She asked me some questions. I paid close attention and answered the questions correctly.

She handed me a teeny tiny piece of steak. I could hardly see it. I was mad. I couldn't control myself. I hit Susan as hard as I could right on the boobies. I knew it would really hurt if I hit her there as opposed to just hitting her on the arm.

Susan screamed, "Ouch," and bent over. Then she left the table. Mommy asked if she was okay. Of course, she wasn't okay. I hit her hard, but she said she was fine. After that, Mommy said we needed to stick to the food rewards cut up as they were. Someday we'd move to a token system, and get rid of so many food rewards, but we never did. At the time of the smaller food rewards problem, Susan had worked with me for about a year. After that, Mommy said we didn't need Susan. Anya, Jessy, and Mommy had "brainstorming meetings" once a month instead of having a consultant. The home program actually became even more interesting after that.

Jessy worked with me on the weekends. Sometimes Mommy and Daddy went out by themselves while Jessy worked with me. After my session with Jessy was over, she stayed in our house for many hours. She played with me and spoke to Mommy and Daddy. Mommy said she was lonely for her family in California. She came to Newtucktin because she received a full scholarship at the university. Otherwise, she would have stayed closer to her family. Mommy was always worried about Jessy when she left our house.

Chapter 16: The Bellyache

Abie's Thoughts

Everything seemed to be going well until I started to feel a knife shoot through my tummy. I don't know how the knife got there. It was painful. I hated it. I knew many words at that time. But I didn't know how to tell Mommy about my bellyache. It hurt so badly I wanted to scream, cry, break things, and hurt everyone around me. I also felt like I needed to go to the bathroom, but when I went to the bathroom, nothing came out. I had many tantrums, and nobody knew why. Not Mommy, Daddy, Anya, or Jessy. I felt like this every day for a very long time... many months. The pain didn't go away even though I wanted it to. Then one day Mommy helped me in the bathroom and noticed I was bleeding. She grabbed her head and started to breathe heavily. Then she said, "Abie, Abie. Are you okay?" I felt bad pain, the throwing up feeling, and my head felt funny. But at that point in time, I was already used to feeling bad. I hated feeling like this. But what could I do about it?

Mommy called many doctors on the telephone. She said, "Abie's bleeding from the rectum. We need to see someone as soon as possible." One doctor's office said I could have an appointment in a year. Mommy called Dr. Treisman's office, and the social worker recommended Dr. Surrelle. When Mommy called Dr. Surrelle, his secretary said I should come in that day. We visited his office, and he recommended a colonoscopy as soon as possible.

Mommy called the Newtucktin Hospital. I heard her screaming at them. "NO, ABIE CANNOT WAIT UNTIL 1PM TO HAVE HIS PROCEDURE. HE HAS TO BE FIRST. HE HAS AUTISM, AND THE PROCEDURE WILL BE NEXT TO IMPOSSIBLE FOR HIM. I DON'T CARE IF THERE ARE YOUNGER CHILDREN TO TAKE CARE OF. THEY DON'T HAVE AN ISSUE LIKE ABIE. HE MUST BE FIRST." She was crying, her face was red, and her hair looked all out of place. Then she hung up the phone and screamed, "What a BITCH!" Then she called Dr. Treisman. While she was talking to Dr. Treisman tears flowed down her cheek and she said, "Oh thank you Dr. Treisman. Please do whatever you can. I appreciate it, and I cannot thank you enough." Dr. Treisman called up three hours later, and then I heard Mommy say, "Thank God, and thank you, Dr. Treisman. I don't know what I would have done without you." Then lots more tears came out of Mommy's eyes.

A colonoscopy is no fun at all. It begins with "prep." All the food in your house disappears except for lemon flavored Gatorade, lemon Italian ices, bullion, and tea. Your mommy forces you to drink something that tastes bad. You are never ever allowed to drink Drano. Nobody is allowed… not real people or retards or animals or anyone else. But for a colonoscopy, you have to drink something like Drano. It drains all the insides of your tummy. Then you get the stomach flu with the throw ups and diarrhea. When you wake up in the morning, your mommy and daddy take you to the most horrible place imaginable….the hospital. Like I said before, when someone mentions the word, "hospital," try to run away fast, and don't come back.

When you first arrive at the hospital, you feel very cold, and hungry, but nobody gives you anything to eat. You might see some people in the hallway with drinks and food, but if you try to take that food, your parents will stop you. Then they put a scratchy name tag on your wrist. It feels like a million knives are cutting into your skin.

The next step is waiting…...and waiting, and waiting, and waiting. You have to wait a very long time, and you wonder if you'll have to stay at the horrible hospital forever. That might make you bite your wrist or hit your mommy. She should have been able to fix this, but she didn't fix it, so she deserves to be whacked. They make you wait in an uncomfortable place with bright noisy lights, and annoying people poking at you. After you've waited so long that you can't stand it any longer, they make you wear special pajamas that open in the back. They do that to make you feel even colder and more uncomfortable. Then a nurse comes by to connect an "ivy" into the insides of your wrist. This ivy is worse than poison ivy and it hurts when they put it in. I tried to rip out the ivy, but Mommy said, "NO" and kept me from doing that. Then she said if I rip it out, they'll put it back in. I didn't want them to do that again so I tried very hard not to rip it out.

I wanted to leave. As soon as I could, I was going to take off. But before I knew it, some people wheeled me into another room. This room was even scarier than dental torture rooms. I knew they were going to hurt me. They may even kill me. I saw Dr. Surrelle there. I thought he was nice, but I must have been wrong. He wanted to put a mask on me to suffocate me to death. I jumped off the bed, and shook my head "no." I screamed and cried, but they kept on trying to get me to let Dr. Surrelle and all of the other mean people to suffocate me. Mommy was in the room too, but she didn't help me escape. I never knew why. She led me back to the bed, and said to lie quietly. Someone said something about the ivy, and suddenly I felt very calm and sleepy. I yawned.

Then a few minutes later I woke up, but I was in another room. There were some other kids in beds too. I wanted to get out of there before they had a chance to do more bad things to me, so I jumped out of bed. Mommy was there, and she said, "Abie, you can't get out of bed. You can't walk straight yet. You're going to fall. Get back in the bed." There was no way I was going to listen to Mommy. I wanted to leave, and I was going to leave. Then I heard a lot of talking, and suddenly Daddy ran in. They both took me back to the bed, and said, "Abie, everything is going to be okay. Do you want some crackers and a drink?"

I was hungry, and the idea of crackers sounded good, so I nodded, "yes." Mommy said I had to stay in the bed until it was okay to get out. They gave me crackers and juice. This was nice, so I thought maybe all the torture was over. I felt a little calmer with Mommy on one side of my bed, and Daddy on the other side of the bed. None of the mean strangers were paying much attention to me while I enjoyed the crackers. Then finally, a nurse came over, poked around me, and said I could get dressed and leave. Mommy took my clothes out from under the bed and closed the curtains. She handed me the clothes one by one, and asked me to put them on. I did each piece without causing any problems. Once I was dressed, I would get to leave that awful place. We left, and I was glad I was finally out of there.

After that day, I screamed and cried every time we drove passed that hospital. I wanted Mommy to know for sure that I never wanted to go there ever again. I had to see Dr. Surrelle in his office at least every six months after that. After about four weeks, the bellyache disappeared, and so did the bleeding. I was much happier after that.

Arlene's Thoughts

Abie's behavior began to deteriorate for some unknown reason. He had many tantrums, but we didn't know why he had them. He also ran back and forth to the bathroom many times. Everybody who worked with him thought that the tantrums were a common issue in individuals with autism. We all thought his visits back and forth to the bathroom were escape behavior. His behavior deteriorated as time went on.

One day Abie went to the bathroom and filled the toilet with blood. He was bleeding from the rectum. When I saw this, I practically passed out. I asked him if he was okay. He repeated, "okay," but I didn't think he knew what he was saying. I cleaned him up, and called the pediatrician right away. He called back, and said he would provide a referral to a gastroenterologist. He gave me some names and said to try to get an appointment as soon as possible.

I called the gastroenterologist who was known to treat kids with autism, but he had a wait list of over a year. I told the secretary that Abie was bleeding from the rectum, but the secretary said, "Sorry. That's the best that I can do." Then I called Dr. Treisman's office. Her staff found a pediatric gastroenterologist, Dr. Barry Surrelle, who could see him right away. We went there the next day. He said we needed to schedule a colonoscopy for Abie right away. Both Jon and I had colonoscopies for years because there was a history of colon cancer in both our families. We knew what that entailed. I didn't see how we could do this with Abie. He would need to clean out his system so Dr. Surrelle could see his colon. That meant a liquid diet for at least 24 hours, taking large doses of vile-tasting laxatives…and a visit to the hospital. The idea of preparing him for a colonoscopy sounded beyond impossible. But what choice did we have?

We didn't ask anyone who worked in our home program to participate in the colonoscopy event. After all, we weren't interested in having anyone quit on us all of a sudden. So I bought the colonoscopy food, and I removed every morsel of food from our house. Abie would have gone through the cabinets to look for food. If we had any, he would have found it while I went to the bathroom or when I got distracted. Our only choice was to remove food from all of the cabinets in our house. Then I bought syringes. If Abie refused to drink the vile laxatives, I had plans to hold his nose and force them down his throat. Luckily, he was willing to drink some of this, but I did have to force some of it down as well.

While we were preparing him, he made nausea sounds, and he went to the bathroom many times. At the end, when his bowel movements started to turn yellow, he whimpered when he went to the bathroom.

I thought he might be up all night because he was so hungry. He had been through hell. However, he slept like a rock as soon as his head hit the pillow that night.

In the morning, we brought him to Newtucktin Hospital. He saw people there with their morning bagels, muffins, and coffee. He lunged to try to swipe someone's bagel. Jon and I restrained him. I wondered how we would do this if we were older and not as strong.

We checked in. A staff person directed us to the waiting room. We waited there at least an hour and a half. I brought a portable video player and a variety of stimmers. Our objective was just to keep him under control until they brought him in. The wait seemed like an eternity.

Finally, they brought us into another room. Abie had to dress in a hospital gown that opened in the back. He was happy to get into the bed and under the covers. He seemed so cold. Then the nurse came by to put in the IV. I turned Abie's head around so he couldn't see what she was doing. He tried to take his arm away. He didn't want the IV, and he let us know. We held him down so that she could put it in. She was finally successful after stabbing him a few times. I saw him going for the IV with his other hand. I held him down, looked into his eyes. "Abie, just leave it alone. If you rip it out, they'll do it again." He seemed to understand my words completely. He pulled his arm back, and laid there with a defeated look on his face. Once the IV was in, we waited another fifteen minutes. It seemed like an eternity. Then they wheeled him into the procedure room. They let me come into the room with him. They wanted to give him anesthesia through a mask over his face. That sent Abie into a panic. He pushed the mask away, and smacked Dr. Surrelle in the face. Abie jumped out of the bed, screamed and tried to escape from the room with his IV still connected. As I led him back to the bed, the team was discussing providing something through the IV to relax him. Within a few minutes, Abie was sleeping. They told me I could leave the room. I could join Jon and see the nurse together. I felt the worst was over, but of course, it wasn't.

"We'll only allow one person in the recovery room. Do you want to be present or do you want your husband to be present?"asked the nurse.

"Abie's going to be in a state of panic when he comes out of anesthesia. He's going to need us both in the recovery room. I don't think I can handle him by myself."

"We have a child life specialist who can help you out in the recovery room. You don't necessarily need your husband. She knows what to do so everything goes smoothly."

"Abie has autism. It's not going to work."

"How do you know it's not going to work?"

"Because we know Abie. We know he needs both of us there. You'll be sorry if you don't have us both in there."

The nurse bristled. "Is that a threat? I don't take kindly to threats. ONLY ONE IN THE RECOVERY ROOM, AND THAT IS FINAL. Your husband can wait in the waiting room."

"Okay. If that's how you want it. Jon will be ready to come in when Abie starts causing problems."

"Don't be ridiculous," the nurse said in a snarky tone of voice. "We'll let you know when he's finished with his procedure. In the meantime, both of you can go to the waiting room."

We went back to the waiting room where we waited and waited. We saw people going in for colonoscopies with other physicians, and we saw them coming out. Then we saw new people going in and coming out. We saw the third shift of patients going in and coming out. I held Jon's hand. I whispered in his ear. "This can't be good. There must be some kind of problem. Something's wrong."

After the longest two hours in my life, someone came out to tell us Abie was in recovery. I was thrilled he was alive after such a long wait. I told Jon to wait by the door. I went to the recovery room.

Abie's eyes were closed. As he opened his eyes halfway, he jumped out of the bed, and tried to run for the door. He must have still been under the influence of the anesthesia. He stumbled around as if he was drunk. The child life specialist came over and said in a perky voice, "Hi there. It's time to get back into the bed." Then she raised her hand, which had a sock puppet on it, and said in a funny voice, "Let's get back to bed, Abie." He pushed her away, and kept on running. I tried to force him back to the bed, but he was too strong for me. Then the nasty nurse ran to find Jon, who was standing just outside the door waiting for the scene to happen. He came in and helped me get him back to bed. We asked for food, which the hospital staff gave us. This calmed him down, and kept him busy in the recovery room.

In the meantime, Dr. Surrelle came by and told us Abie had lesions in his colon he needed to biopsy. That was why the colonoscopy took so long. He said it looked like Abie had Crohn's disease. This was what was causing the bleeding.

Wasn't it enough that Abie had autism? Couldn't this diagnosis have gone to someone else who didn't already have a battle to wage?

At least Abie had a diagnosis. We knew what was bothering him, and we knew what to do about it. Dr. Surrelle gave Abie medication, and within a month, all bleeding stopped. Abie was happier. His problems with tantrums and escape faded as his Crohn's went into remission.

The medication we gave Abie were four large capsules four times daily. On the package, the instructions said not to break the capsules. There was no way we were going to get four unbroken capsules into Abie. So I ignored the instructions and broke the capsules. Then I hid the medication in his food. I hoped this way of delivering the medication would be temporary. I was overwhelmed at the thought of having to teach Abie how to take his medication, but help was on the way.

We notified the Behavioral School that Abie had been diagnosed with Crohns. The nurses at the school called me soon after that.

They assured me they were going to teach Abie to take his capsules. They took this very seriously. Over the course of about four months, they taught Abie to take the capsules by offering him pieces of pizza as a reward. It had been a long time since I was able to trace a newly learned skill to the Behavioral School. They did a great job. I was grateful. He learned to take his medication easily, without protest, and he swallowed the capsules whole. These nurses were seasoned employees who knew exactly what they were doing. After Abie learned to take his medication, the nurses either left the Behavioral School or were let go. Young, inexperienced nurses took their places. Abie was the last student who learned how to take his meds from these nurses. The new nurses did not get involved with medication taking issues.

Chapter 17: Nature's Cruel Joke

Abie's Thoughts

A few months after I had my fourteenth birthday party, I noticed certain things happening to my body. Odd-looking hair appeared in strange places on my body. Hair started growing on my face. First Mommy shaved my face one a week, then twice a week, then four times a week, and finally almost every day. She tried to teach me to shave my own face. I wanted to, but I kept missing giant spots on my face. Shaving was too hard, so I just wanted her to do it for me.

Some animals have a tail in their back. But I have a tail in my front. I pee out of this tail. I noticed when I woke up in the morning, my tail was hard and I couldn't pee until it softened up a little. Sometimes some slippery liquid stuff would come out. Was that some special kind of pee? Sometimes the pee comes out, and sometimes this other stuff comes out. How does one come out, and how does the other come out?

Sometimes I feel like I want and need something, but I don't know what it is. This feeling was the strongest when I was a teenager. This feeling had something to do with all of the changes I had.

The changes in my body had something to do with becoming a grown up. Mommy told me that. That's why I like her. She tells me things even though I'm a PDD uneducable low functioning autistic retard who is not supposed to understand anything anybody says. Nobody else ever mentioned anything about what was happening. It was no use to speak to me because I didn't know how to show them I understood what they were saying.

I wouldn't become a real grown up. Instead, I would become a retard grown up. That means I'd still be a kid, but I'd have a body like a grown up. I didn't want that. I wanted to be a real grown up. I wanted to go to work, have a wife, and not have other people always telling me what to do. If I couldn't do that, I wanted to just stay a kid.

One day when I spoke to Mommy and Daddy, I had to look down at them. I realized they were little, and I was big…much bigger than they were. That made me happy. I also noticed the teachers and the teachers' bosses who were so bossy and bossed me around were also little, and I was big. I was way bigger and stronger than they were. So why were they telling me what to do instead of me telling them what to do?

Life was confusing before all of this happened. After that, it was even more confusing.

I also started to like rubbing my tail up and down. I especially liked to put slippery soap on my tail and rub it in the bathtub. Mommy always walked out of the bathroom when I did this. She made me go in my room when she saw me doing this. She said it was private, and I had to do this in my room. I wonder why.

Arlene's Thoughts

Running Abie's home programming was like running a business. There was always something to troubleshoot or organize. That became my more than full time job. The flexible intensive services grant paid for all Abie's home services.

PCPP Educational Services did nothing to help manage or organize the service. The only responsibility they took seriously was generating checks for our workers. PCPP's cut was a third of the money the DMR allotted to us. I complained to Katie Norsbeth that PCPP Educational Services was not providing what they promised. Katie said she could help arrange a switch to another provider. Otherwise, she couldn't help me. I thought about doing that, but there was always a possibility that PCPP might find some staff. With the other agencies, they clearly expressed that I must find, train, manage, and supervise my own staffing. I couldn't find enough staff to use up the money anyway...so it didn't matter that the agency was price gouging.

In one way, the flexible intensive services were the best thing that happened educationally to Abie. He progressed steadily, and seemed to understand more and more of the world. He understood much of what we said to him. He began to follow directions that weren't specifically taught to him. He spoke more and more in his whispery and inarticulate voice. He began to do simple chores like sorting flatware.

Abie never developed play behavior. At age fourteen, the time for that had passed. Too bad he didn't have his age fourteen skills when he was age four. Maybe if he did, the schools wouldn't have written him off so quickly. If only time could stand still while Abie caught up!

Then, one day, I spied a pubic hair on Abie as I helped him with his bath.

I went into a state of panic that day, but it was no use. In the days, weeks, and months to come, he started growing fuzz on his face and more pubic hair on his privates.

Noooo! No! This couldn't be. He's a baby. How could this happen? How could I stop this? This has to be a mistake.

It seemed like he grew an inch a day. Before we knew it, his shoulders were broad and muscular, and he towered over us.

I suppose the parents of typical kids find puberty a little

disconcerting also. However, they can look to the future with pride as their children showed the characteristics of the adults they would become. For us, puberty just seemed to be a cruel trick that God and nature played on Abie for no apparent reason.

If Abie were typical, Jon would have taught him how to shave. It would have been a rite of passage on the road to manhood. Instead, I shaved him. I tried to teach him to shave independently, but it was no use. He couldn't do it.

Poor Abie! I don't think that he understood what was happening to him. He was probably bewildered and frustrated at all the changes we couldn't stop from happening.

I wondered as I watched Abie change. Would we be able to hire workers for our home program as time went on? Would the tiny women who worked with Abie still be willing to work for someone who was beginning to look like a man? How would we take Abie out in public? He needed supervision in the bathroom. Could we continue to take him into the women's rest room? Would I need to find men who were willing to care for him in public? Where would I find men to do this?

I tried to will his puberty to progress slowly. *Please, please, please, oh pubic hair, please don't grow! Don't grow so tall! Don't grow so muscular and broad! Stop it! Stop it!* But I couldn't stop it. He went into puberty at age 14. This was the normal age for a boy to go through puberty. It was not abnormal. It was inevitable.

Puberty for Abie was the foreshadowing of the adult he would never become. He'd sleep alone for all his days. He'd always need help. No wonder his behavior began to deteriorate at times. Maybe in some way he understood the sadness of it all.

Chapter 18: Friendship

Arlene's Thoughts

After working for us for two years, Anya was going leave us and PCPP Educational Services. She found another career opportunity with benefits and a chance for advancement. Jessy was going to graduate and move back to California. Abie inspired her to study neuroscience for her graduate degree. Her goal for her future was to help more children like Abie. I kept hounding PCPP Educational Services to send us prospective candidates to replace Anya and Jessy. I was getting tired of chasing down Craig Miller to find us workers.

One day, much to my delighted surprise, PCPP Educational Services sent us Campbell Graham's resume. She had ten years autism experience in an adult-serving agency. Her resume boasted a director of clinical services job title. She said she could handle any behavior under any circumstance. She claimed to have experience in working with the most behaviorally challenged individuals in the entire state. This was impressive... so I hired her.

After she passed her criminal background check, I called her and asked when she could start. She was available the next afternoon. I wanted to pick up a prescription for Jon at the pharmacy. I left her with Abie, but I took my cell in case she needed to reach me. It took about ten minutes before she called my cell to tell me she couldn't handle Abie. "He has some very odd behaviors. He can't speak clearly. He's difficult to engage." I wondered if she had listened to my description of Abie during our interview. She certainly didn't sound like she had the vast experience with autism she claimed.

I turned my car around, and went back to the house.

Campbell was sitting in a chair while Abie was running wild taking everything out of the cabinets. "I can't work with Abie. I quit. I'm pregnant, and I don't want to work with anyone who has a history of maladaptive behavior."

She lasted exactly twenty minutes on the job. I chastised myself for not calling her employer to verify the truthfulness of her resume; but surely, I thought PCPP checked her out.

Then PCPP Educational Services sent me Margot Trenwall. Margot had no experience with individuals with disabilities at all. She claimed she wanted to learn, but she totally ignored Abie during her interview. She wore a variety of bling which seemed distracting to Abie. I told her frankly, "It's going to take a lot of work to train you. I need a commitment of at least a year in order to consider hiring you."

"Absolutely, I'll give you one year's commitment minimum."

"Are you willing to commit to that here and now?"

She smiled. "Oh, yes, definitely."

"Okay, then I'll try you out." I called PCPP Educational Services and told them to go ahead. After all, I had no other prospects. Then Craig Miller told me, "Margot decided she's not interested in working with children with autism. Sorry."

I called Mary Carpenter to tell her PCPP Educational Services couldn't find us a therapist. I wanted to make certain PCPP didn't bill the school system for services they weren't delivering. I didn't complain about noncompliance with the IEP to the Department of Education. I just let it drop. That was the end of home programming the school provided. If I ever found someone to work, I could just charge it to the flexible intensive services. I had plenty of funding, but no personnel.

I put an advertisement in at the university's student employment office. I received a resume from a young student named Natalie Hughes. Natalie had worked with children with special needs, but had no autism training. She was interested in learning about verbal behavior. I sent her to verbal behavior trainings, and I worked side by side with her for about three months.

She got better and better at working with Abie. After three months, it was time for her to take the reins, and for me to fade back into the background. What a relief!

One sunny afternoon after she finally went solo with working with Abie, she brought him to the park after school. When she arrived back at my house, she told me she met some people I knew at the park. The people she met were Darlene Diamond, Matt, and Matt's home therapist, Casey. Two weeks later, Natalie quit working for us and started working for Darlene Diamond. Natalie worked for us for about three and a half months. She had been out of training for just two weeks when she left us. I trained her, my flexible intensive services grant paid for outside training for her, and Darlene Diamond reaped the benefits.

In response to another ad I placed at the university, I received a resume from a young student named Jason Croft. Jason also had some special needs experience, but no autism experience. After the Natalie and Margot fiasco, I didn't want to repeat what I had done before. I didn't respond to the resume. Finally, Jason emailed me and asked if I would be willing to meet with him. I had nothing to lose, so I set up an appointment ....even though I made up my mind that the answer was "no."

146

I invited Jason in. He immediately went over to say "hello" to Abie. He gave him a high five. Then he asked Abie to sit with us. That was certainly new. He continued talking not to me, but to Abie, "So Abie, do you want to hang out with me? We could do fun things like throw balls and go out for pizza. Then we could listen to music and watch TV. It'll be fun…just hanging out. I can teach you some cool things. What do you think?"

Abie looked at me with a smile and nodded his head "yes." I was shocked he knew what was going on. Abie had made up his mind. He trailed behind Jason like he was the Pied Piper. He wanted to hire Jason.

"Jason, do you have any experience with children with autism?"

"No, I don't. I did have some experience as a counselor-in-training in a special needs camp, but none of those kids had autism."

"Jason, what are you studying in college?"

"I'm a trumpet player. I'm hopeful I'll be one of the few who actually make music a career."

"Why do you want this job?"

"I don't know. I can pick up a few extra bucks I need while helping a special needs kid. It sounds like a good job."

I liked Jason Croft, and so did Abie. I didn't know about spending a lot of time training him in verbal behavior. It wasn't going to help him in his career as a trumpet player.

"Jason, would you consider being a respite worker rather than a home therapist? I'll pay you a little less, but autism experience wouldn't be essential. You could watch TV, go out for pizza, and hang out..just like you told Abie."

"Sure, I'll take what I can get, and it sounds fun."

"Okay, you're hired."

The following Saturday evening Jason took care of Abie while Jon and I went to a movie. It felt so luxurious just to do something for just Jon and me. It reminded me of years ago when Jon and I were dating. No worries. Nobody to take care of. A true break. Well…..not exactly, I spent some of the time worrying about how

Abie would do with Jason. After all, Jason had no autism experience.

When we walked in the house after our "date," Abie was still up with Jason. They had just finished eating ice cream sundaes and Jason was spinning Abie around while he was laughing. Jason offered to help Abie get ready for bed. I accepted his offer.

Abie and Jason were friends. The relationship was uneven...and yes, I paid Jason, but they were pals, nevertheless. I had practically given up on the idea that Abie would ever know friendship, but I was wrong. After Jason put Abie to bed, I offered him some tea which he gladly accepted.

I thought about all the activities Jason could be doing instead of hanging out with a disabled adolescent and his parents. "Jason, wouldn't you rather be out with your buddies or chasing young women than spending your time with us?"

"Not really. It was nice to come here and be with Abie. I had fun."

"Thank you so much. It looks like Abie had a wonderful time."

"Yeah, that's why I wanted the job."

After the first two years of flexible intensive services, I hired many people, trained many people, and did a lot of filling in with working with Abie myself. It was an unbelievable amount of work. I imagined it might actually be less work just to do all the therapy myself without the help.

From the time Abie was diagnosed, my whole world really consisted of Abie and his needs. Jon and I did not have any semblance of a normal life. He had to work hard to support us financially. I did some advocacy on the side, but it didn't really provide an income. I couldn't work, and run Abie's home program at the same time. Plus there was no daycare for someone like Abie, and my staffing for the home program was less than reliable. I missed going into an office and working. Jon had a retirement account, but I didn't. If I were working, I could accumulate money to help secure our future. There were also many things I longed to do, but I couldn't. I would have loved to invite people over for a dinner party.....but that was impossible with Abie around. I missed having a neat and clean house. Even having a hobby was impossible. My life was Abie, and only Abie. It was easy for me to see why so many parents of disabled children end up getting divorced. There was no time to nurture a relationship. If it weren't for people like Jason Croft and Maureen Pauley, Jon and I would never have been able to partake in any leisure activity ever. They kept our heads above the water. Otherwise, we would have drown into the abyss.

Abie's Thoughts

Anya said she was leaving my home program. It didn't matter to me because every time she came to the home program, she left and went home. So leaving was nothing special. After all, she always came back the following Monday, Wednesday, or Friday. I didn't know this leaving was different from her normal leaving. When she said she was leaving, I said, "bye." I liked Anya because I spent a lot of time with her. She was a part of my life. When it was Monday, the time for Anya to work with me, Mommy worked with me instead. I liked working with Mommy, but Anya was supposed to work with me on Mondays, not Mommy. I wouldn't do what she asked, and I had a meltdown. Then the following Wednesday came, and Anya still wasn't there. I bashed in a wall, and tore a lighting fixture from the ceiling. By the time Friday came and Anya didn't come, I got the idea that Anya was never coming back. Maybe she was dead like Sean's sister. The teacher told him his sister went to a place called "Heaven" and she wasn't coming back. He pointed to a picture of his sister all day in his communication book, but she never came back. So I guess that teacher was right.

Then Jessy said she was going to leave too. By then I figured out what that meant, so I got angry and bit my wrist. I wondered if Mommy and Daddy would leave also. Then what would I do?

After Jessy and Anya left my home program, I had many teachers who came for a short time and then left. I didn't like any of them. Some of them didn't talk directly to me unless they were doing work with me or Mommy told them to. They were boring, and not very interested in being with me. Then Jason came to our house. He talked directly to me. I don't think he knew I was a PDD uneducable low functioning autistic retard. Nobody told him I was. I hoped he would be my new babysitter even though I wasn't a baby, and nobody who babysat me ever got a chance to sit. Mommy hired him. He came on Saturday nights when Mommy and Daddy went out on a date. We had more fun than they did because we went out for pizza and ice cream. I don't think Mommy and Daddy ate any food on their dates. If they did, they didn't talk about it.

Chapter 19: Residential Placement

Arlene's Thoughts

One Monday morning, I received an unexpected call from Patricia Stone, who was now the CEO of the Behavioral School. Over the years, the Behavioral School grew to serve over 500 individuals. There were now fifteen vice presidents, and numerous directors and managers. I hardly ever received a call from Patricia anymore. At first I thought, "maybe there's some emergency with Abie." She assured me there was no emergency, but she had some excellent news for me. I wondered what this could be.

"Mrs. Dancer, we have some wonderful news for you. We have an opening in a group home, and Abie is an ideal candidate to fill that slot."

My eyes almost popped out of my head. I never expressed an interest in a residential placement. I was doing everything I could to avoid it by working hard at staffing and managing our home program. "Patricia, I'm surprised. I never actually inquired about a residential placement."

"I guess you got lucky. We have evaluations from Dr. Treisman over a period of five years. Each one of them states that Abie needs 24/7 education and care. With the right lawyer, you should have no trouble obtaining funding from your school district for a residential placement."

"We're trying to provide the 24/7 education and care via the flexible intensive services program."

"You've inquired several times at the school for respite workers and therapists. Wouldn't it be nice not to constantly look for staff?"

I did inquire at the school, but somehow we were never able to hire a single therapist or respite worker from there since Maureen Pauley. I figured there must have been an unspoken rule against employees working for the families of a student. Anyway, Patricia struck a chord. Yes, I did think it would have been nice not to have to continuously hire and train so many people... especially when PCPP Educational Services was actually getting paid to do this.

"I never actually considered a residential placement for Abie. This is sudden for us."

"If you don't place Abie in residential while he's still eligible for school services, his chances of being serviced by the DMR in a group home setting at age 22 becomes quite bleak. You're able to care for Abie now. Think about whether you'll be able to do this when you are 70 or 80 years old. You might have your own health problems then. If you don't secure a residential placement before Abie is age 22, the DMR might not serve him residentially until you die or are terminally ill."

I knew residential services were quite lucrative for the corporate special education schools. They had a spot to fill, and I had a kid who could fill it. However, I heard this same story about how vital it was to get a residential placement while the school district still covered him. Many children of parents I knew were going into residential placements at Abie's age or younger.

I pleaded, "Abie is 15 years old now. What if I waited until he's 18 years old?"

"That's the point, Mrs. Dancer. We like to get our students into residential placements as early as possible. We want to train them early so they do well in our highly structured and rigorous programming. If we wait too long, they'll lag behind the other students. Also, at age 18, we probably won't have an opening. We like to accept children ages 10-15. Actually, age 15 is the cut off. If you don't take this opening, it's unlikely you'll be able to place Abie residentially here. It's also unlikely you'd be able to place him residentially anywhere else. Private specialty schools tend to take their own day students. The other schools are also inclined to take children ages 10-15."

"Aside from the risk of not getting into residential when he turns an adult, are there any other ramifications if we don't agree to take this residential placement?"

"Officially, no. But we need to fill this spot with someone in our day program. If we don't, we'll have to take someone from our wait list. When a new student takes the residential component, we'll also need a slot for him in the day program. We'll have to take appropriate steps to make sure we have that available."

I got her drift. Abie would be kicked out of the school if we didn't accept this. I thought this would be the case, but I wanted to hear it from her. I had to think fast in order to stall her. "I need to talk this over with my husband. In the meantime, let's set up an appointment to see the group home."

When Jon came home, I told him about the phone call from Patricia. He said we had no choice. If we didn't take this opening, she would find a way to get Abie out of the school to make room for someone who'd take the residential slot. We knew she was also correct about getting a group home placement while he was still served under the school district.

Jon seemed to age ten years within the hour I spoke to him about this. We agreed to sleep on the decision.

That night I awoke when I heard a huge thump in the night. I turned over and saw that Jon was not there in the bed lying beside me. Then I saw him lying on the floor. He looked like he was dead. I ran over to him in a panic, and shouted, "JON! JON! WAKE UP. WAKE UP." He didn't wake up or stir. He was limp. I tried to feel if he was still breathing and had a pulse. He did, but he wasn't moving. He was unresponsive. Thoughts swirled in my head. *Call an ambulance. Get him to a hospital.* Then I thought again. *He'll go in the ambulance to the hospital all alone. He'll stay there in the hospital by himself until Abie goes off to school at 8 am. I have nobody I can call in the middle of the night to come and help us. What if Jon died in the hospital without my being there?* Then suddenly Jon came to and moaned, "Arlene, I'm okay. I just fainted. I'm fine. This might be a side effect from medication. I'll call the doctor in the morning. Let's go back to sleep." The tears flowed from my eyes. I made my decision about Abie... a cruel decision... a decision that no mother should ever have to make about her vulnerable son.

Patricia had arranged for us to view the group home when nobody was there. She said viewing the group home when it was in operation was a HIPAA privacy violation. That was a red flag. I ignored it though. What else could I do? When we viewed the house, it was neat and orderly. I wondered what actually went on when residents were there.

I called Mary Carpenter. I asked for the residential placement. I wanted to secure the placement without spending money on a lawyer. I had the right pieces of paper, and I knew what I had to do. "Mary, I'm calling about Abie. There's an opening in a group home at the Behavioral School. We're interested in that opening."

"Oh, I see. We can have a meeting with the school to figure this out. I knew this day would come."

At the meeting, we talked about adjustments to the IEP for a residential component. The school district didn't fight the residential placement at all. Mary Carpenter didn't say a word against it. After all the fighting we did to get services to help Abie improve, this was the service the school district handed us on a silver platter. However, I knew we were lucky. Some families had to spend their life savings on legal help to secure a residential placement.

154

I called Katie Norsbeth from the DMR, and told her our decision. "Flexible intensive services delayed your decision to place Abie residentially by a few years. That's something," said Katie.

Nobody ever asked us what kinds of supports we would need to keep Abie living at home. We could have kept him at home. If the DMR provided a guarantee of care and housing when we were old and could no longer able to care for him....if we had a good school placement close to our home... if we had trained staff at home... if we had someone to call in an emergency... so many elusive ifs! These "ifs" would have cost a fraction of a residential placement. But the system does what it does, and can't do what it doesn't do....and that's that. It doesn't matter if the only feasible option tears families apart. It is what it is.

I called our home therapists to tell them Abie was going residential. We no longer needed their services. They had only been with us a short time, and few of them were planning to leave soon anyway. The only one I told in person was Jason Croft.

Jason started crying when I told him. "How can you do this to Abie? Why can't he live with you?"

Indeed, I thought, *how could we do this to Abie*?

"Jason, someday, we're not going to be around. He needs to get used to having other caregivers. He'll still come home on the weekends and other occasions," I said.

"Could I still babysit him?"

"We appreciate your asking, but we'll lose our flexible intensive services funding once he goes residential. Since he won't be seeing us the whole week, we want him to be with us when he visits on the weekend. Jason, you have talent with working with people like Abie. I'll find you another job working for another family."

"I'm not upset because I'm losing my job. I'm upset because you aren't fighting for Abie anymore. You've given up." Tears rolled down his cheeks, and his voice cracked.

"We'll never give up on Abie. NEVER EVER. No matter what happens. We just need more help. That's all."

A very sad Jason left our house that night. I spent only a half an hour on the telephone, and I was able to find a lovely family who needed a good respite worker. There were many parents looking for someone like Jason. I knew that someday, he was going to make one heck of a great father.

I arranged for Abie to move into his group home on a Thursday. That way I could pick him up the following Friday for a home visit to see how he was getting along. Despite our best efforts and despite noticeable gains, he was nowhere near the point where we could dream he would be able to live independently. He needed to get used to the way it would be once his parents could no longer look out for him. This was his reality.

Abie's Thoughts

I was a bad boy…a terrible boy who caused a lot of trouble. I didn't have quiet hands and feet. I broke many things including walls and light fixtures. I stole food off other people's plates, and pillows and blankets too. That's why I wasn't allowed to live with my parents anymore. That's why I couldn't hang out with my pal, Jason Croft. Instead of being in my own bed with my own pillow, I had to live in a noisy house with seven other retards. Instead of having my own room, I shared my room with a boy who stimmed all night and gave me a whack whenever he felt like it. I had to sit on vinyl chairs that made my tushy and back sweaty instead of Mommy's comfy couch. I lived in a house with a locked refrigerator, and locked up cabinets. The staff decided when I could eat, where I could go, what I could do, when I could take a shower, and how long that shower would be. I was in jail for all the terrible crimes I committed.

I wondered if they would ever let me out. I hated my life. Nobody ever spoke to me except to order me around. They thought I was too stupid to understand what they were saying, so they didn't bother. They spoke about me while I was right there listening.

There were four staff in the Oak Grove group home…so that's a total of twelve people in a house built for four. It was crowded, messy, noisy, smelly, dirty, and confusing. None of the staff there responded when I spoke in my whispery voice. I was all alone. Abandoned.

Nobody cleaned the bathroom. The staff had a private bathroom in the house so they never had to use that retard bathroom. The bathroom we used had pee and poop all over it. It smelled. Instead of having a bath whenever I wanted, I got timed for a two minute shower. They gave my clothes to other retards, and they put someone else's clothes on me. I couldn't keep my own clothes anymore even though Mommy sewed labels in them with my name on them. This was annoying because the too large pants fell down, and the too tight pants were uncomfortable. Instead of eating Mommy's delicious home cooking, I got my food out of a can or I ate spaghetti and stale white bread. Instead of having people who worked with me with intensive teaching, we just sat around, stimmed, or watched TV. Then the TV broke and we didn't even have that.

I just wanted to block it out, and retreat into my own world. When they first dropped me off there, I didn't know if I'd ever see Mommy and Daddy again or if they abandoned me there forever. I wanted to shout and scream at them, "Please don't leave me here." But I couldn't. Tears came out of my eyes at night when I thought about Mommy and Daddy leaving me here.

Then on Friday, Mommy came to pick me up. I felt relieved when I saw her. She didn't throw me away. She didn't forget me.

She took me to the car. As she took me, I saw that tears were dripping down her eyes. As soon as she brought me into the house, she immediately brought me to the tub. She helped me wash my hair, helped me shave, and had me dress in fresh clean clothes. She did this every Friday when she picked me. She told Daddy she didn't think that I had a chance to get clean. She told him they weren't taking care of me.

As soon as I came into the house, I smelled all of the familiar smells. Challah bread baking in the oven. Roast chicken with onions. I smelled the cake Mommy had baked. This is what Jewish people call "Shabbat." In addition to being a PDD uneducable low functioning autistic retard, I'm also a Jewish boy. This is a good thing. This means I eat matzoh on Passover, and I eat hamantashen on Purim. Best of all, this means I visit my parents on Shabbat even though they made me live in a group home. I waited every day for Shabbat to happen. Some real people don't like the Jewish. They say so right in front of me because they think I don't understand what they are saying. They don't know that being Jewish is a good thing.

At home visits, Mommy tried to get me to talk and understand the world and learn new things. Also, I got a chance to eat the food Mommy cooked, sit on the comfy couch, and sleep in my bed with five pillows. Whenever she picked me up, I thought that she might keep me home forever, but she always took me back to the Oak Grove group home. I made a fuss whenever I had to go back to the group home, but it was no use. She always took me back there.

Chapter 20: Sinking into the New Normal

Arlene's Thoughts

We began to settle into our sad new lives. There was no question that Abie was regressing in the residential placement....especially his oral speech. His case manager at the Behavioral School said they were concentrating on the communication book, but I never saw him initiate communication with the communication book. All his attempts at initiating communication were with oral speech or using gestures. He hated using the communication book. He didn't like scanning the pictures. He hated turning the pages and hunting to find the one item he wanted. I suspected that nobody spoke to Abie all week long except to give him orders. I imagined him living each day in silent isolation until we rescued him on the weekend.

Abie's behavior also began to deteriorate. I had never seen him so angry, even when he was suffering from a Crohn's flare. I felt nervous when he was alone with me. I thought he could hurt me. We ended up putting him on antipsychotic medication to control his aggressions and self-injurious behavior. I didn't blame him for his bad behavior. He had every right to be angry.

His acne got increasingly worse. I didn't believe they kept him clean or took care of his skin. His stress levels probably didn't help the acne either.

In the most diplomatic way possible, I tried to talk to the school about some of these issues in the group home. I had to walk on eggshells because the threat of termination always loomed large in the background. I never made any headway with these advocacy efforts. I was a good advocate, but I was only good when it came to advocating for more services or different services. I couldn't affect the quality of services for anybody, only the quantity. I was forever on the lookout for a possible alternative placement for Abie.

When Abie was young, I hoped he could lead a normal life. After age five, I hoped he would reach his own potential. After age seven, I hoped he would just have some nominal improvement. Now my hope was...someday I could take him out of his placement and get him into a better place.

However hard it was when Abie came to visit us, it was a thousand times worse when he wasn't with us. Our house was bustling with activity when he lived at home. Without him, it was silent and empty. It felt like the walls of our home were crying with sadness and grief. The baby I prayed for, the son who I would do anything for, the confused teenager who I longed to help, was now in the care of others. The folks who cared for him in the group home were all recent college graduates. None of them had any children. They earned a ten dollar an hour wage. Most were merely biding their time until they got a better job. Some of them cared about the individuals they served, and others didn't appear to care at all. All of them came and went with the regular beat of cruel employee turnover. None of them loved Abie the way we did.

Dozens of times a day I felt like packing up Abie's things and bringing him home. Then I thought about the practicality of doing that, and I changed my mind.

As I faced what my life had become, I decided it was time to go back into the workforce. I needed something else to think about other than what I had done to Abie. Grief and guilt would get the better of me if I didn't replace it with some other things to think about.

It was time to secure our future retirement. I put my moping aside and started striving for what I longed to do for the fifteen long years since Abie's birth.

I could have continued to do special education advocacy. I would have needed to promote my services in order to get more clients and work more hours. The thought of dealing with the school systems full time made me nauseous. I needed to get away from special education and the system. I needed a break from it.

I had a bachelor of science in management with a concentration in marketing. Before Abie was born, I worked as an office manager at the registrar's office at the university. I also did some research for an information broker and wrote some abstracts for a business publisher. My skill set was fifteen years old. Much had changed since before Abie was born. When I left the work force, everyone used IBM Selectric typewriters and index cards. This was different from cubicle jungles, powerful computers, email, and internet that I faced.

I thought about going back to school for an advanced degree. However, I wasn't certain I could make up the cost of getting another degree. I was way behind with taking fifteen years off to raise Abie.

In the end, I decided to update my skill set, and look for any job I could get. My goal was to get Microsoft Office Specialist certifications. I studied on my own. Once I passed the Microsoft tests, I could prove I had an updated skill set. Being self-taught was advantageous to a prospective employer. I wasn't afraid to learn new technologies when the need arose. A prospective employer might be impressed that I had hired, trained, supervised, and managed staff in Abie's home program. It was no small task to design and monitor his curriculum and organize the program. A mother of a severely autistic child works 24/7. There's no break. What employer wouldn't want a workhorse like that?

It isn't unusual for parents of children with special needs to have troubles in the workplace. Many must leave their jobs in order to care for and advocate for their special child. The longer the time off to raise the child, the harder it is to re-enter the workforce.

So instead of constantly designing and updating a curriculum for Abie, I worked on a curriculum for myself. Every day I woke up early to begin my studying routine. I read encyclopedic reference books, watched videos, and practiced problems in Microsoft Office applications. I didn't stop until I knew what every feature in every menu could do. I was always learning new and creative ways to use these tools to solve problems. I passed the Microsoft tests, and proudly added "Certified Microsoft Office Specialist" to my resume. After three months of intensively updating my skill set, I was ready. I could handle most problems that might come up in an office environment. I also lost fifty-five pounds to look more presentable.

I applied for every job I was qualified to do. I wanted a job as a data analyst using Excel. I applied for those jobs. I also applied for office manager, administrative assistant, marketing, and other managerial positions. I wasn't fussy. I was willing to take any salary and any job that would make use of a subset of my skills. I sent out over 200 resumes, and went on twenty-four interviews.

My job search taught me several lessons. First, there was no greater sin than having had a special needs child to take care of. This meant you have baggage. When interviewers asked about the hole in my resume, they didn't want to hear about my advocacy work for my son and others, and they didn't want to hear about running a home program for an autistic child. Some expressed an interest in my Microsoft certifications, but couldn't consider me because I had no real life work experience in these applications at an actual job.

The blow to my self-esteem was sharp and cruel. In my mind, everyone else in the workforce DID have better skills than me.

Managing the unmanageable and doing the impossible had no possible application in the workforce. The interviewers insinuated this, so after a while I began to think that they were right.

Connections are everything. After a year of searching, through a friend of a friend of Jon's, I was finally able to land a position as an administrative assistant with an adult human services provider called BeyondCareCorp. This provider served adults with intellectual disabilities as well as the mentally ill and some other populations.

I was thrilled to get this job. I thought it might give me a window into what adult services were like. I might learn how to advocate for services when Abie reached age 22.

On my first day of work, the parking lot at BeyondCareCorp was crowded. It was difficult to find a space. There were several reserved spaces for the CEO, the CFO, the VPs, and several directors. In these reserved spaces, I saw some Lexuses, Acuras, BMWs, and at least one Jaguar. In the other spaces, I saw a wide variety of older jalopies, tin Lizzys and some subcompact cars. I guess my ancient Chevy Cavalier station wagon fit right in. I stopped taking my car in after the first day. Like most rank and file employees, I took public transportation instead.

I always believed people who worked in human services earned lowly wages. I was soon to learn at BeyondCareCorp, this held true only for the folks at the bottom of the totem pole, and especially the direct care workers. There were plenty of highly paid, wealthy BeyondCareCorp executives.

BeyondCareCorp advocated for competitive employment for individuals with intellectual disabilities. They fiercely advocated for the closure of sheltered workshops and other "isolating" environments such as developmental centers.

I looked forward to observing how the staff at corporate headquarters interacted with the individuals with disabilities.

I noticed how my office and my boss's office were so neat and clean. The carpet was vacuumed perfectly, the windows shone, and there was not a speck of dust around. I was impressed. *Were folks with disabilities on the cleaning staff? What other jobs would people with disabilities have in the company?* I assumed people with disabilities would be very visible in that environment. I couldn't have been more wrong in my assumptions.

The cleaning staff came from a contracted cleaning service. There were no cleaners with intellectual disabilities. There was not a soul with a disability found on the premises of the corporate headquarters. BeyondCareCorp could have been a company manufacturing widgets. Few employees in the corporate headquarters held any interest at all in individuals with disabilities.

At a meeting, I once suggested the company consider having some of the individuals they serve do the cleaning in the corporate office. The executives at the meeting explained to me, "You are here to take notes, not to express your opinions." Then later, a colleague said to me, "Do you really want retards cleaning your office? Are you nuts? Don't you enjoy having a nice clean office?"

"I do want people with disabilities to have jobs. It's disingenuous of the company to advocate for competitive employment for people with disabilities when the corporate office wouldn't think of hiring anyone from this population."

"That's ridiculous! I've never heard anything so stupid. You don't have to worry about that anymore. We have a person like that working here. YOU!" Then she turned on her heel and walked away.

Other than the attitudes of the staff towards people with disabilities, I liked my job. It turned out that I had far more expertise in Microsoft Office applications than anyone else I met at the company. My colleagues frequently lined up outside the door of my office. They waited there for my help on their Excel problems. I felt good about helping those people. I felt useful...just like when I taught Abie something. When I helped them, I felt Abie's presence in the room. I saw his smile, and felt his soul. This brought me joy. It was all about Abie.

My boss's boss at BeyondCareCorp, a highly paid executive, was one of the people I helped the most. He didn't understand how to use files and folders on a computer. This made it impossible for him to store and retrieve information. I made it my mission to teach him how to do this. He wanted me to store his files, and retrieve them for him. Just like Abie preferred that I zipped up his jacket when he was perfectly capable of doing that himself. I couldn't understand how anyone could function in the modern office environment without knowing about files and folders. I tried repeatedly to teach him, but either the uptake of information or the motivation to learn was not there. This reminded me of teaching Abie, and the frustration I felt when I couldn't reach him.

The challenges in the workforce could never compare to the challenges I faced as Abie's mom. Even with office politics and everything that came with it, work was just a heck of a lot easier than being Abie's mom.

After two years as an administrative assistant at BeyondCareCorp, I was able to land a job as a data analyst at another company.

Abie's Thoughts

I didn't like being in the retard group home, but after a while, I got used to it. I was able to block out everything bad by stimming. That helped me cope with the situation. I liked retreating into my own world. Sometimes I thought Mommy would get me out of the Behavioral School and group home. She was always talking to Daddy about doing that.

There were times when I was happy there. There were teachers I liked. Whenever anyone had a birthday, we had cake and ice cream. I liked that too. So from time to time, it wasn't all bad, but it wasn't like being with Mommy and Daddy. But, whenever I felt sad and alone, I thought about Mommy and Daddy, and that made me feel better. Sometimes if I thought hard enough, it felt like Mommy was in the room with me. I imagined her coming to my bed, telling me "good night," and kissing me on the forehead.

I needed to think about Mommy being in my room to protect me because I shared my room with Don. He was the one who gave me a whack whenever he felt like it. One night Don woke up and bit me on the shoulder for no reason. I woke up and screamed because of this.

During the day and part of the night, there were four staff people bossing us retards. Sometimes the staff people were boys, sometimes girls. In the middle of the night, all the staff went home, and two small and skinny girls came for the "the graveyard shift." They call it the "graveyard shift" because it's supposed to be quiet with everyone sleeping. A graveyard is quiet because all the people in a graveyard are dead. Dead people can be in two places at once. All dead people are in either heaven or hell, and they can be in a hole in the ground in a graveyard too. Good people get to go to heaven, which is wonderful, and bad people go to hell, which is terrible. All retards are bad, so all retards go to hell.

One of the skinny girls cleaned my bite wound from Don, and wrote something in a book. She told the other girl that someone was going to call my mother the next day.

The next night I woke up and heard terrible screaming. Billy was on the toilet and Don was going after Billy. He was biting him, hitting him, and kicking him. The two skinny staff girls were hiding in a corner. They were scared. Billy was screaming and screaming, but nobody did anything about it. Don was hurting Billy bad, but he didn't know how to fight back. Don't blame me for not helping because I didn't know what to do either. I just wanted it to stop.

Some of the other retards woke up. They walked around, but mostly they stayed away. They were scared too.

Finally, Billy fell off the toilet. He fell to the floor like he was falling asleep. Blood was gushing out of many places of his body. His mouth was open and blood was coming out of it. Then Don ran back into our room, and one of the skinny girls shut the door of the room with me outside it and Don inside it. She held the door shut so Don couldn't get out. Then the other skinny girl called an ambulance on the telephone. Some people came in, and put Billy on a bed they carried around. They called this "a stretcher," but it didn't stretch. Then they carried him into a van with a red light. It had the worst sound you could imagine. I covered my ears tight when I heard that sound. Another van came and took Don away too.

One skinny girl told me to go back into my room and go to sleep. I went back into the room, but all the walls were broken. Clothes and other things were on the floor. A dresser was lying on its side. Plaster was everywhere.

I went back into my bed, but there was plaster in my bed. There was also some broken glass on the floor. I guess Don bashed in the window. The skinny girl came in later; taped up the window; and cleaned up the glass. The next morning I went to school. There was plaster dust on my clothes. I was coughing a lot.

After I came back from school, someone had cleaned things up a bit, but it took about a week until it was back to normal.

After a few days, Don's mother came to get his things. Tears were gushing out of her eyes the whole time. She was making sounds like that cat did when a car hit it. Her eyes were red and her face was red. When I looked at her, tears came out of my eyes too, and I felt something unhappy. I didn't understand it, but I knew I felt this way because of Don's mom. I never saw Don again. I got a different roommate. The two skinny girls who worked the graveyard shift left after two weeks. I never saw them again, but two new skinny girls started the graveyard shift instead.

Billy came back to the group home after a week. He had bites and scratches all over him, a big black eye, bumps and black and blue marks all over his face and arms. One arm was in a piece of cloth that was tied to his neck and shoulder. He cried every half hour or so. He was afraid to sit on the toilet in the night after that, so he peed in his bed. Because Billy peed in his bed, he never had to have a roommate. So I peed in my bed too. I hoped I would get my own room that way, but I didn't. They just let the pee dry, and that was that.

Chapter 21: Outrageous

Darlene Diamond's Thoughts

Can you believe all of the garbage that Arlene Dancer is saying? Only the best and kindest people go into special education and human services. They go into these fields because they want to help the disabled. Period. Nobody goes into human services for money or power. I never heard anything so ridiculous! Professionals in these fields don't make much money. Executives in business earn several million dollars, not the measly six figure salaries they earn in special education or human services. Instead of complaining about their high salaries, she should be thanking them for all of their service, hard work, and dedication to people with disabilities.

She should be grateful, but yet, she has the nerve to complain about award-winning schools and providers, the DMR, the school system, the healthcare system, and even other parents of children with disabilities such as myself.

Patricia Stone is one of the most respected and wonderful people I have ever met. She's won awards, published articles, and has spoken all over the world. She's done so much for my son and for

Arlene's son as well. Arlene is lucky her son received such a wonderful education there. The taxpayers paid a lot of money for her son's education. It isn't the Behavioral School's fault her son is low functioning and cannot learn. They did their best with what they had.

Mary Carpenter is wonderful too. I never had a problem with her. Early intervention was a godsend. They saved my son.

When my son went into adult services, BeyondCareCorp got him a job at a pharmacy retail chain. They got him a regular part time job in competitive employment. So what if it wasn't at their corporate office? I also used PCPP Educational Services for my son, and I had no trouble at all getting the best staffing for my son's home program.

What has Arlene Dancer done that she should be so high and mighty and criticize everyone? She never stepped up to the plate to be on the parent advisory committee at the Behavioral School as I did. She was lazy in advocating for her son and incompetent at running her son's home program. Some advocate! She never contributed one bit to the disability community. How dare she criticize others, especially people who are champions for those with disabilities?

Part 2: BATTLE OF AUTISTIC ADULTHOOD

Chapter 22: Beyond the Cliff

Abie's Thoughts

I visited Dr. Surrelle for nine years. I saw him every time I had a tummy ache. If I didn't have a tummy ache, I still saw him at least every six months. I punched him in the face once, and I kicked a dent into his desk during an office visit. Once I got into some of his papers and I made them fly in the air.

I got crumbs all over Dr. Surrelle's office because Mommy gave me graham crackers for waiting nicely...except I didn't wait nicely. Once Mommy gave me a juice box, and I saved it in my cheeks. Then, when I saw Dr. Surrelle, I spit the whole thing into his face.

I disturbed his patients in the waiting room. I turned up the volume on the Disney Movie on my DVD player. Mommy wanted me to wear headphones, but I didn't want to feel the headphones on my ears.

If you think I was bad, Mommy was even worse than me. She made me look well-behaved in comparison. She read on the internet that some people with Crohn's disease had to have their colons removed. I don't know what a colon is, so that didn't bother me. She cried and cried in Dr. Surrelle's office, and then she begged him not to remove my colon. Dr. Surrelle said my Crohn's was mild, and I might never need such a treatment. He also said people who have their colons removed learn how to deal with it. That made her cry more. She said those people probably didn't have autism. He told her not to worry about that… because I had done very well. I'm not sure what I did well. It probably wasn't my behavior.

Mommy called Dr. Surrelle every time I acted badly. She never knew if my behavior was a result of Crohn's disease or a result of autism. She was always worried I would start bleeding from the rectum, and I would have the problems I had before.

I visited Dr. Surrelle right before I graduated the Behavioral School. This was a visit like no other visit. Dr. Surrelle's face was red, and tears were coming out of his eyes. He said to my mother in a voice that was cracking, "Abie's no longer a kid. He's getting too old to see a pediatric gastroenterologist. It's not fair to him to keep seeing me at this point. He needs an adult physician who is educated and experienced in the issues adults have. If he ever needs a procedure, he has to be in an adult unit at the hospital, not in a pediatric unit. If you need help finding an adult gastroenterologist, I'll help you find one. It's time for Abie to move on. I'm going to miss him. Actually, I'll miss you both. I'll never forget this experience. It's been a pleasure and a privilege. Thank you for that."

Dr. Surrelle wasn't happy to see us go. I wonder why. Shouldn't he have been celebrating that he wouldn't have to deal with us anymore?

Arlene's Thoughts

The Department of Mental Retardation changed their name to the Department of Developmental Services or DDS. Departments all over the country were doing this. The term "mental retardation" had a negative connotation. People connected this term with the pejorative "retard." I hate the word "retard." Nobody should ever use that word. However, it would have been better to spend money on services rather than a name change.

Abie was in residential services at the Behavioral School for more than six years before he became eligible for DDS adult services. He was at the Behavioral School for seventeen years in total.

Most other parents I knew were dreading the day their child was no longer eligible for children's services. Jayne Johnson and other parents called this, "falling off a cliff." It sounded ominous, but all I knew was that Abie was finally getting out. Getting out was what I had hoped and prayed for since he was five years old. My hope and wish was finally coming true.

The Behavioral School conducted workshops on "Turning 22" to help families understand what was coming next. In these workshops, Patricia Stone and others explained how the adult system worked. They advised the parents to look at as many adult programs as possible. Behavioral Enterprises, now the parent company of the Behavioral School, ran adult services as well children's services. Jayne Johnson had her son in their adult services, but she was unhappy. I wasn't interested in using the Behavioral Enterprises's adult services in the least. I had been dreaming of getting out for years.

The DDS determines if a given intellectually disabled individual is a priority for assistance. They give the parents a form that takes an inventory of the individual's activities of daily living skills. The school fills out a similar form to see if the responses match. After that, an evaluator tests the individual's IQ.

I didn't know what to expect, so I was nervous about the IQ testing. On the day of the testing, I met the DDS evaluator, Guy Marfuto, at the Behavioral School. He seemed nice. He greeted Abie directly, but Abie didn't respond. Guy had some items in his bag he used for IQ testing. Together, we brought Abie into the testing room. I wanted Abie to do well on the IQ test because he was so much smarter than everyone thought. I also wanted him to do poorly on the IQ test so he'd get the services he needed. I'm not sure how I could want those two conflicting things at the same time, but I did.

Guy asked Abie to do various tasks to test his IQ, but Abie wouldn't comply at all. I suggested Guy use food rewards or stimmers to get him to comply.

"I'm going to classify Abie as Priority 1, which is our highest priority. He's always going to need a lot of assistance. His IQ number is "untestable."

Abie was eligible for a day program and a group home. The DDS considered him to be in their top priority category. They thought he was so impaired that he couldn't even be tested. At least we jumped over the first hurdle easily. The next step was to find an appropriate day program and group home. This proved to be more difficult.

Some of the programs I saw were just bad. One program served sixty individuals, but only had two sinks and toilets. That was inappropriate for a person with Crohn's disease, who needed quick access to the bathroom. Many programs resembled nursing homes with people just sitting around and doing nothing.

There were also providers who told me I could not see any of their programs because of HIPAA privacy rules. If they weren't proud of the program enough to want to show me, there was definitely something wrong, and I wasn't interested.

Some of the programs were good, but I couldn't picture Abie there. Many of them were designed for individuals with Down's syndrome. Some providers didn't know anything about autism. I later learned the system was designed to serve individuals with Down's syndrome. It hadn't changed with the changing population needs.

For adult services, I worked with a new DDS service coordinator named Annie Painter. When Abie was only six months from his twenty-second birthday, she said it was too early to look at programs for him. She refused to refer us to any programming. I was afraid the DDS was just going to place Abie anywhere convenient for them regardless of whether it was appropriate.

Abie had "vocational skills" on his IEP for over a decade. I figured it was worth a try to ask Annie about a job for him. After all, the DDS claimed they focused on "employment first." Annie summarily dismissed the idea of him working. He was too low functioning, did not stay on task, and had behaviors. At that time, sheltered workshops still existed. However, self-advocates, advocacy organizations, and others were fighting hard to get rid of them. Abie wasn't really a candidate for competitive employment, so his chances of ever being employed died along with the closure of the sheltered workshops.

Abie's twenty-second birthday was fast approaching. I was getting nervous…maybe there was no program to be had at all.

I spoke to Guy Marfuto. He suggested I look at Peoplefriends, Inc. They specialized in autism.

One afternoon, Jayne Johnson and I took a trip to visit them. They were about an hour away from my home. The director of social services, Caroline Jones, met with us and explained the features of the program. Then we toured the facility. Caroline said they were in the process of moving, so the facility would be different going forward. Unfortunately, the new facility was also an hour away from my house.

They were a behavioral program, but they didn't seem quite as rigid as the Behavioral School or the New Progress School. This program was the most promising program that I saw. They also had a small and relatively unknown children's program. Immediately I regretted I didn't know about them previously. Perhaps I would have been able to get Abie out of the Behavioral School sooner.

I liked Caroline Jones. She explained the provider's philosophy, but didn't go on and on about how wonderful they were, and how lucky we would be if they accepted us. After years in the special education system, I was finally able to discern someone who feigned empathy versus someone who really had empathy. Caroline Jones was someone who had a heart. This was a good sign. Peoplefriends would not be perfect, but I did get a good feeling. Jayne confirmed my feelings, but she wasn't ready to uproot her own son from his placement at Behavioral Enterprises. I decided immediately this was going to be the program for Abie. I went back a second time with Jon. He confirmed Peoplefriends was probably the right choice.

I called Annie Painter the next day and told her we wanted Peoplefriends. She told me the Brooktin Corporation had an opening for someone turning age 22. I had seen Brooktin Corporation, and it wasn't a specialty program for autism. I was sure they wouldn't be able to handle Abie. Peoplefriends had no opening for Abie.

"If you want an autism specialty program, we could refer you to the Behavioral Enterprise's adult services," she said.

I was stuck once again. "These options aren't going to work."

"This is the best I can do at this point. You have to choose from those two options."

I felt like I had the rug pulled out from under me. I wanted Abie to be out of the Behavioral School for years. I couldn't stomach either of the options presented to me.

Adult services were different from children's services. There were no entitlements, and all the laws were different. I needed help. I hired a support broker named Deb. A support broker is responsible for assisting with the development and implementation of a person-centered plan. A Person-Centered Plan or PCP focuses on the strengths, interests, and needs of an individual. Deb was expensive to hire, but Jon and I couldn't do this by ourselves.

The idea of a person-centered- plan sounded silly to me. The DDS decided what services each individual received. They and the corporate providers decided whether the individual would be working, doing activities, learning something, or just sitting around. A person-centered plan seemed extremely far from what the reality actually was. The individual got what those in charge wanted to give him, and that was that.

However, Deb's advice was sound. She wanted us to appeal to the emotions of Annie's boss, Loretta. "Create a PowerPoint presentation about Abie and his likes and needs. Show cute pictures of him. Make Loretta want to do something for him."

Deb's strategy might work with some people, but it wouldn't have worked with Mary Carpenter or Patricia Stone. I was leery.

On the day of our meeting with Loretta, we struggled to find the district office of the DDS. It was behind a bend that was out of sight and was extremely difficult to find. We were nervous we wouldn't find it in time for the meeting. Jon's hand was shaking so much that I needed to carry the laptop with the PowerPoint on it. We met Deb in the parking lot. She was good for moral support. We couldn't deal with being there by ourselves. We were scared, anxious, and overwhelmed. Loretta had the power to either make our dream come true, or to kill our hopes.

I convinced myself to calm down, and do what I set out to do. I would just do my best. I felt myself forcing a smile and telling Loretta, "Pleased to meet you." I pulled out the laptop, and went through my PowerPoint presentation, which had a charismatic and smiling Abie doing all sorts of household tasks on each slide.

Loretta's face told me she enjoyed the PowerPoint. "There's one opening in a group home at Peoplefriends, but it isn't a clinical match for Abie. He would have to be there temporarily until Peoplefriends opened another group home. It might take about a year until he gets into his permanent placement," she said

I couldn't believe my ears. I looked at Jon. He nodded. Then I said, "Yes, we want to see the opening. That might work. Thank you so much!" Tears flowed past my cheeks, and I noticed that Jon was crying also.

So as friends and relatives saw their children graduate college, launch their careers, get married, or go on to graduate school, our dream of getting Abie out of a school placement that didn't work for him actually came true.

Abie's Thoughts

Mommy and Daddy brought me to a house on Trubb Street. It was a long drive, and I couldn't understand why they brought me there. What was in that house? Would they hurt me there? Would it be loud in there? Would it smell? I made up my mind. I was NOT going in. Then Mommy said they had some food in there for me. Then I thought, "Maybe going in might not be so bad." I was still nervous, my hand trembled, and I walked behind Mommy just in case. I put my face into her shoulder.

Inside was a normal house, but it had some old retards in it. One man could have been a hundred years old. Another man couldn't see because he was blind and autistic. He had a music room in the basement with thousands of CDs. He put the CDs away after he listened to them. It looked like he had a spot for each CD in a pile or on a bookshelf.

Later when the staff gave me lunch, I realized the blind guy could play the piano and the guitar perfectly. He could find any CD and put it back in its original spot, but he couldn't eat with a fork and knife. Somebody had to feed him.

I went to the Trubb Street house several times. One time I had chicken there. Another time I had a sandwich. I stole food from the blind man. It was all too easy because he couldn't see and I knew it.

Mommy said this was my new group home. I was going to live there after my twenty-second birthday. How could that be? I already had a bed in a group home. I didn't understand.

The staff at the Trubb Street was chocolate, and they came from the same place that Sebastian the crab did. Sebastian took care of the little mermaid, Ariel, because she didn't do what her father told her to do. I need to have people taking care of me because I don't do what my father says to do either. Sebastian spoke funny because he was born far away. The staff at Trubb Street must have come from the same place as Sebastian because they sounded just like him when they spoke. They speak that way in the Caribbean and a place called Africa. Shakira sings a song about Africa called *Waka Waka*. "Waka Waka" sounds like stim noises, but when real people sing, it isn't counted as stim noises.

I visited Trubb Street, and the staff from Trubb Street also visited me at the Behavioral School. They called this "transition."

On the day of my twenty-second birthday, my parents came to pick me up at the Behavioral School. I wanted to go home right away because I always want to go home right away. However, this time they took me into a room. There were many snacks laid out on a table. They were playing loud music. There was a big cake on the table. I saw the words, "Congratulations, Abie!" on the cake. Usually I like party food and cake, but I was ready to leave. My parents were there, and I wanted my hot bath followed by a nice meal made by Mommy. The loud sounds hurt my ears. There were too many people in the room.

"Don't you want a piece of your graduation cake?" Mommy asked. I shook my head "no." I ran out of the room without saying good-bye. My parents followed me. We went into the car, drove away, and I never saw the Behavioral School or anyone who ever worked there ever again.

That night I slept at Mommy and Daddy's house. The next day I went to a new school called a "dayhab." The following day, I moved into the house on Trubb Street. I finally had my own room, and didn't have to worry anymore about a roommate. The house on Trubb Street was much quieter than my previous group home, even though the old man retard had some very loud stim sounds. There were only five of us at the Trubb Street house with two staff. After a year at Trubb Street, I moved to another group home on Michael Street. There were four of us there along with two staff. It was even quieter there. I felt relaxed when the van took me there after a day at the dayhab.

Chapter 23: In the Community

Arlene's Thoughts

Newtucktin had a large Jewish population. Within a six-block radius of my house, there were seven synagogues. When Abie first received his diagnosis of autism, we were living right across the street from a large synagogue. We joined this synagogue when we bought our first house, and had been members for five years before Abie received his diagnosis.

The rabbi had a great reputation. A family whose young daughter had suffered with leukemia recommended him. "He's kind and compassionate," they said. He helped them deal with an awful situation.

Spiritual guidance, compassion, and a caring community was just what Jon and I needed. So around the time of the diagnosis, I called Rabbi Coheny. The synagogue had a many resources including a full time social worker. There were supports for the elderly, the sick, and for people in mourning. Surely, there had to be something there for us.

I'll never forget the conversation I had with that rabbi.

"Rabbi, things aren't going so well for us. Our son has been diagnosed with autism. I'd like to talk to you about that."

"I'm so sorry to hear about that, but I'm not sure why you're contacting me. I don't think there's anything we can offer you."

"I'd like to talk to you about the diagnosis, and perhaps talk about possible ideas for Jewish education. I want to discuss including him in our community."

"You need to talk to the education experts rather than us. He needs intervention, not religion. Have you been in touch with early intervention?"

"Why, yes, of course! But I wanted to talk specifically about inclusion in the Jewish community."

"Our religious school isn't equipped to educate someone diagnosed with autism or mental retardation, or even something milder like dyslexia. We just don't have those types of resources. I do know a little bit about people with mental retardation. I can to tell you about an experience that I had. I once went to an interfaith conference at the Brooktin Corporation. Are you familiar with the Brooktin Corporation?"

"Yes, of course."

"Well, anyway, I went to an interfaith conference in the Brooktin Corporation's facility. The mentally retarded people there made lasagna for us. It was delicious lasagna. Maybe someday, Abie will be the one making that lasagna. So there's always hope."

The conversation was leading nowhere. I didn't want to accept the fact that the synagogue was not going to be a support for us. So I said, "maybe we should set something up so that we can talk face-to-face."

"Sure, if that's what you want. I'll transfer your call to my secretary, and she can set something up."

"I was wondering if you could possibly come here. I don't have anyone to watch Abie, and I don't think it would be good to bring him to your office."

"No, definitely, don't bring him here. Please feel free to call back at a time when you can come without him."

"Couldn't you come to my house? After all, it's right across the street."

"No, I usually don't do that. Occasionally I'll visit a house of mourning, but that's it. I'm pretty busy, and unfortunately, I can't accommodate something like that."

So that was that.

Like many religious communities at that time, the Newtucktin Jewish community shut out children with disabilities and pretended they didn't exist. There was no effort to include them in Jewish education, synagogue life, recreational activities, or anything else. There was no help, no natural supports, and no compassionate community. However, there were parents and advocates who wanted to change things for the better, and they did. As time went on, there blossomed an impressive array of programs and activities for children with disabilities. One philanthropist made it his family's mission to include disabled in the Jewish community. This was a good thing... but not for us.

When Abie received his diagnosis, we had to deal with the fact that there was no place for our son in the Jewish community. Then a few years later, we had a new array of programs designated for children with disabilities which would reject us. The programs created were for higher functioning individuals without any behavioral issues, not for someone like Abie.

Somehow, some disability advocates think housing people with disabilities in the community will somehow magically make them part of it. The community can be every bit as isolating as an institution when the community is unwilling to accept the disabled. When I worked at BeyondCareCorp, every group home we opened meant there would be a fight with the neighbors.

Going on field trips in the community is not the same as being part of a community. Being part of a community means people say "hello" to you on the street. They know you, and they care about you. This can only happen when individuals with disabilities are given appropriate community based instruction, and when a community is willing to accept people with disabilities even when it is difficult to do so.

For many years, we just ignored this situation with the Jewish community. After all, we had friends and relatives who pretended Abie didn't exist as well. So we weren't exactly strangers to that line of thinking.

However, as the community began to change for the better, it did get better for us. Although we never benefitted directly from the efforts of Jewish advocates for the disabled, we did benefit indirectly. As time went on, the community began to believe that people with disabilities SHOULD be included in the Jewish community even though some of them weren't. We began to see a change of attitude.

Then Jon's father died. He went to various synagogues in the area to say Kaddish, a Jewish prayer recited in the daily ritual of the synagogue and by mourners at public services after the death of a close relative. He liked going to a small synagogue that met in a rabbi's house. This rabbi said Abie would certainly be welcome there.

Jon said to bring Abie after services, right in time for the food. He would be too disruptive during prayers.

I had nothing to lose, so I decided to try it. Neighbors began to know who Abie was. They greeted him when I took him for walks in the neighborhood. He began to respond to others greeting him. This had a positive impact on him.

Chapter 24: Never Die

Arlene's Thoughts

As soon as we had a paid up house and enough money in the bank to live on, Jon and I retired. We had been under pressure our entire married life. When we found a route to take that would make life easier, we took it.

As the years passed, many of Abie's maladaptive behaviors subsided, then disappeared. It is hard to believe such a gentle, sweet soul as Abie once had aggressive, self-injurious, and destructive behavior. People who work with him are shocked that this is in his history. He still has problems and is quite impaired, but he's pleasant to be with, and very happy. I often wonder whether his unhappiness during his school years caused those behaviors.

Abie's ability to read remains a secret. Nobody ever discovered it, and I never thought it would benefit him to tell anyone about it.

I'm now a senior citizen...an older woman. There are wrinkles, sags, flab, and gray roots. I attend too many funerals. I know my time will run out too. If I don't feel old enough by looking in the mirror, I can just look at Abie. His hairline is receding, and he has a few wrinkles too. He's thirty years old, the age I was when we received his autism diagnosis.

Taking care of a person with autism never stops. I can never retire from this job. I can never die because I know I'm irreplaceable. Yet I know I will die someday.

There is still way too much to do. There is always advocacy that needs to get done or something I must teach him. This is true even though he lives in a group home.

Abie's Thoughts

Today is Monday. Today has to pass, then Tuesday, then Wednesday, then Thursday, and then on Friday, I get to see my Mommy and Daddy. They are mine. They belong to me, and not to anyone else in the dayhab or the Michael Street group home. When I see them, I'm the happiest, and when I don't see them, I think about when they will come.

Chapter 25: A Worthwhile Life

Arlene's Thoughts

The other day I met Miriam Goldman at the supermarket. Her son, who went to Harvard, just fathered his second child with her beautiful, smart, and fantastic daughter-in-law. Her children and grandchildren are extremely gifted. Her daughter is in her last year of medical school and is the best in her class. She can go on and on about her life, while completely oblivious as to how that sounds to a person who has struggled. It doesn't matter. I'm happy for her. Miriam is living her life, and I'm living mine. She was meant to take one journey, and I was meant to take another. Her journey led her to the point where she is bragging about how wonderful her life is to someone like me. My journey has led me to another place.

I never did cure Abie, but he did learn and progress. He's a very lovable and likeable person. He never made any money or paid any taxes, but he's done some very important things in his life. He inspired goodness and giving in Maureen Pauley, Jason Croft, Elsa Dubion, Candy, Julie, Anya, and others including Jon and me. He motivated Jessy to go into the field of neuroscience. He gave Drs. Levine, Surrelle, and Treisman a sense of purpose and contribution. He gave a neighborhood and community the strength to do what is right in accepting and including someone like him.

He gave and is still giving Jon and me happiness whenever he learns something new.

Abie's Thoughts

So you see, Mommy was never able to cure me from autism. She and Daddy spent many hours working with me. Although I never got cured, I did learn many things. I learned to talk in my whispery voice and communicate with words, signs, gestures, and my iPad. I learned to dress myself and do chores. I learned to laugh with people and enjoy their company. I figured out how to learn even more from watching movies and TV. Most of all, I learned to act nice except for the times that I steal food from other people's plates. I learned that Mommy and Daddy love me. I can love them and other people back. That is why when my parents come to pick me up, I smile so wide that it takes up my whole face, and I jump up and down with happiness.

Abie and Arlene's Thoughts

So did we win the autism war? You decide.

Q & A with the author, Irene Tanzman

Why did you write this story as fiction?
I wanted to write a book about autism, and I wanted to include the point of view of someone with severe autism who could not communicate. The only way I could do that was through fiction.

How much of this story is true?
The story of my life with my son, Isaac, inspired this story. However, the book contains both large and small fabrications to make the story more focused and interesting to the reader.
I draw from my real life experiences. For example, early intervention provided Isaac with only one hour of intervention per week, and the school system wanted to continue that one hour a week service. This was a shameful offering for a child who had this type of impairment even at that time.

What did you hope to accomplish in writing this book?
Most of the autism books that I have read are formulaic in the following way:

1. The child is diagnosed with autism.
2. The parents are devastated.
3. The parents find a miraculous treatment.
4. The child recovers or has an amazing improvement.

While those types of books are interesting to read, that is not what most autism families experience. I wanted to write a book that describes the true challenges we face.

The book criticizes the system? Didn't the system help your son?
I am grateful for the help our family received. However, dealing with the system was and still is more difficult for us than dealing with Isaac's autism. I look forward to lawmakers, policymakers, and advocates rectifying this someday.

Some professionals in this story are evil. Do you believe professionals in this field are evil?
I have met professionals who are loving, caring, helpful, dedicated, kind, and competent. Some professionals on our journey wanted to help Isaac, and some were successful in doing so. Someday I would like to write a story celebrating those professionals. This book was about the hardships families and individuals face. One hardship is dealing with professionals similar to those described in this book.

You use the word "retard" many times in this book. Why?
This pejorative illustrates discrimination and hate against a very innocent population in our society. It is just plain wrong to use that word ever. I wanted to illustrate the hurt this causes when these victims of hate internalize this horrible word.

Do you believe that someone can cure a child with autism?
With intensive early intervention, I believe a tiny fraction of children diagnosed with autism can function within the normal range. I also believe intensive intervention delivered by a skillful person will help most children and adults with autism.

Is a cure for autism desirable? Shouldn't we accept people with autism as they are?

There are people who carry a diagnosis of autism who look nothing like the classic autism I know. For these people who communicate and function well in society, I believe acceptance is the best course. However, a person with severe, classic autism needs intervention and instruction. Otherwise, the problem will get worse as more maladaptive behaviors take over. I believe this population needs lifelong instruction and intervention.

How has the system changed from when your son was in school?

The most important advancement is the passing of certain laws in many states requiring insurance to pay for autism treatment. Many families now have home programming, a service I fought very hard to get. When Isaac was young, there were fewer autism programs within the public school setting. Now those options exist. This allows those children to go to school in their own communities. The public school denied Isaac access. I believe it might be different today.

Do you believe ABA is beneficial for this population?

ABA or applied behavior analysis is a method used to eliminate or curtail maladaptive behaviors, and help with skill acquisition. This method can be very useful for individuals diagnosed with autism. I am a fan of using ABA, and especially ABA based on verbal behavior, which is ABA for the acquisition of language. Some ABA programs and services needlessly employ cruel and abusive techniques. That doesn't have to be the case.

Are you against the closure of the sheltered workshops?

The ideal is competitive employment, but that is unrealistic for some individuals. The closure of sheltered workshops meant putting people who needed that type of environment out of the workforce. In general, I don't believe removing services promotes inclusion. Only community based instruction, and more community opportunities promote inclusion.

What can faith-based communities do to include individuals with severe disabilities and/or behavioral difficulties?

The goal for individuals with severe disabilities and/or behavioral difficulties is life-long integration within their faith-based or secular communities. The objectives should be to help these individuals learn the skills they need in order to make true inclusion happen. Someone like our character, Abie Dancer, needs to have faith-based and other community activities integrated into his life. These activities need to be life-long connections, not a class or activity that ends once the individual turns a certain age or when the parents die.

Continue the conversation: #AbieandArlenesAutismWar

Tweet your comments @itanzman

Many thanks to Autism Sprinter (www.autismsprinter.org). Please visit them on Facebook, and be sure to like, share, and donate.

Also, please support the following organizations. They advocate for individuals and families affected by severe autism::

National Council on Severe Autism- www.ncsautism.org

VOR- https://vor.net/

The Massachusetts Coalition of Families and Advocates- https://cofar.org/

ABOUT THE AUTHOR

Irene Tanzman, a former healthcare program administrator and data analyst, is a staunch advocate for individuals with intellectual disabilities and autism. She is the mother of two adults, one of whom is diagnosed with autism. She blogs on topics of healthcare, advocacy, and disability.

She is also the author of *Adventures of an Altruistic Narcissist*.